The Kidnapped
Christmas Bride

The Kidnapped Christmas Bride

A TAMING OF THE SHEENANS NOVELLA

JANE PORTER

TULE
PUBLISHING

Chapter One

I T WAS QUIET in the truck.

The kind of quiet that made Trey know trouble was brewing. And if anyone knew trouble, it was he, Trey Sheenan, voted least likely to succeed (at anything legal, moral, or responsible) his senior year at Marietta High.

At eighteen, he'd been proud of his reputation. It'd been hard earned, with rides in the back of sheriffs' cars, visits to court, trips to juvenile hall, and later, extended stays at Montana's delightful Pine Hills, where bad boys were sent to be sorted out. *Reformed.*

It hadn't worked.

Trey Sheenan was so bad there was no sorting him out. Maybe back then he hadn't wanted to be sorted out, and so he'd continued his wild ways, elevating trouble to an art form, growing from a hot-headed teenager with zero self-control, to a hot-headed man with questionable self-control.

Now at thirty-six, after four years in Montana's correctional system, he was tired of trouble and sick of his reputation.

Just hours ago he'd been paroled, a whole year early. It'd come as a shock when the warden came to him early this morning, letting him know that he was being released today. Trey knew his brothers had been working on getting him released early for good behavior, as Trey had become a model inmate (at least after the first year), and the back bone of the prison system's successful MCE Ranch, but he'd never imagined he'd be out now. In time for Christmas.

It gave him pause. Made him hope. Fueled his resolve to sort things out with McKenna.

He missed her and his boy TJ so much that he felt dead inside. But now he was out, coming home. Finally he had the opportunity to make things right.

"It was sure good to see you step outside those gates," Troy said, breaking the silence.

Trey nodded, remembering the moment he'd spotted Troy standing outside the prison entrance in front of his big black SUV. He'd nearly smiled. And then when Troy clapped him in a big hard bear hug, Trey's eyes had stung.

It'd been a long time since he'd been hugged by anyone. A long time since he'd felt like anything, or anyone.

Prison had done the trick, breaking him down, hollowing him out, teaching him humility and gratitude.

Humility and gratitude, along with loneliness, shame and pain.

His dad had died while he was at Deer Lodge, last

March. He hadn't been allowed to attend the funeral. Talk about pain.

He shifted ever so slightly in the passenger seat and flexed his right foot to ease the tension building inside of him, aware that Troy might not actually be looking at him, but he was keeping him in his peripheral vision. Smart. You didn't let a Sheenan out of your sight. Especially not Trey the Dangerous. Trey the Destroyer. Hadn't he even tattooed that on the inside of his bicep on his nineteenth birthday? What a joke he'd been.

What an ass he'd become.

"Should hit Bozeman in thirty minutes or so," Troy said.

Trey said nothing.

"Want to stop for anything? Need anything?"

Trey shook his head. Silence descended. Troy ran a hand over his jaw. It really was too quiet in the truck, what with the volume down on the Sirius radio station, muffling the country songs, making the lyrics an annoying mumbo jumbo, so that the only other sound was the salted asphalt of I-90 beneath the tires, and the windshield wiper blades swishing back and forth, resolutely batting away the falling snow.

He itched to lean forward and turn up the radio volume, but it wasn't his truck and he didn't want to be demanding. He needed to prove to his family and community that he wasn't the hot-head Sheenan that intimidated and destroyed, but a man who protected. He was ready to show everyone who he really was. A solid, responsible man, a *good man*, who was committed to making things right.

And the first person he had to see was McKenna. He was dying to see her, and TJ. It'd been a long time since he'd seen either of them. Two years and a month almost to the day. It had been Thanksgiving weekend the last time he saw TJ, his son. The boy was three. McKenna had been so very silent and sad, sad in a different way than he'd seen before. He hadn't realized that would be their last visit. He hadn't realized she'd decided then that she was through…

He winced at the hot lance of pain shooting through him.

It'd taken him a long time to process that she wasn't coming back. In the beginning of his incarceration, she came every two weeks with the baby. And then gradually she came once a month and then every five to six weeks until that last trip for Thanksgiving when she never returned again.

He'd about lost his mind at Deer Lodge. He'd died in ways you couldn't explain.

She wouldn't write him back. She wouldn't visit. She just…cut him out.

That was when he truly suffered. That was when prison became a living hell. He was trapped. Hostage. He couldn't do anything about it but write and write and write…

He must have made a sound because Troy suddenly looked at him, brow creased. "You doing okay?"

Trey clamped his jaw tight and shoved all the worry and

fear deep down into that tough hard heart of his and snapped the lid, locking it, containing it.

He wouldn't let guilt and anxiety get the best of him.

He'd sort it out. Make it work. There was only one girl for him, one family, and that was McKenna and TJ.

But he had put her through hell. He was the first to admit that he'd done her wrong. She didn't deserve any of the pain and heartache he'd given her... the trouble he'd dished out in spades.

So he had one task: fix the mess he'd made of their lives.

Tonight, tomorrow, sometime this week after he'd cleaned up and calmed himself down, he was going to go to her and apologize for his stupid asinine immature self and beg her forgiveness and show her he was different. *Changed.*

She'd see that he'd finally grown up, and he was ready to be the husband she deserved. Ready to be the father TJ needed and a real family at last.

A wedding, a honeymoon, more kids, the whole bit. He couldn't wait, either.

"Worried about going home?" Troy asked, breaking the silence.

"No," Trey said roughly, his voice a deep, raw rasp. He winced at the sound of it, but what did you expect? He hadn't talked much the past four years. He'd never been a big communicator to start with, but prison just put the silent in him.

"Home for Christmas," Troy said.

"Yeah." And it would be nice. He'd missed the ranch. Marietta. Everyone.

But mostly he'd missed McKenna and his boy.

Just thinking about her and TJ made his gut burn, and his bones ache. Their memory was a pain that never went away.

He dug the heel of his foot into the floor and pressed his shoulder blades against the seat back, pinning himself to the black leather.

Warden and his officers might think it was their excellent corrections program that had turned him around, but it wasn't the work program, or the ranch, or the counseling. It was losing McKenna.

They'd been together for years, since high school. Well, they'd been together off and on for years, but in the months—or years—they were off, there had never been another woman he'd loved. Sure, he'd screwed a few. He was a Sheenan and Sheenans weren't saints, but he'd never cheated on her when they were together.

He'd rather cut his dick off than betray his woman that way.

And then his conscience scraped and whispered, just like the windshield wiper blades working the glass.

You betrayed her in other ways, though.

The drinking. The fighting. The small bar fights. The big bar fights.

And finally, the afternoon at the Wolf Den that changed everything...

"You've been home for a few days now?" Trey asked his twin, wanting to find out about McKenna and not sure how because Troy hadn't brought her up, nor had he mentioned TJ, and Troy always talked about the five year old, wanting to keep Trey in the loop.

"A week."

"What's it like without Dad around?"

"Quiet." Troy hesitated. "It's just Dillon there at the ranch, you know. I'm still dividing my time between San Francisco and Marietta, and when I am here, I'm usually at The Graff."

"Things still good with your little librarian?"

"Yeah."

"Wedding date set?"

"We're talking February, maybe around Valentine's Day since we were paired up for that ball. But things are kind of hairy at work and I'm honestly not sure a February wedding would be the best thing."

"How hairy is hairy?"

"Got hit with a big lawsuit. It should sort out but its damned expensive and time consuming until then."

"Then wait till it's settled to marry. No sense being all stressed out over a wedding."

"I agree." Troy tapped his hand on the steering wheel and then exhaled. "There are some other things going on, too. Family things." He shot a quick glance in Trey's direction. "Dad was a real bastard when it came to Mom."

"That's not news."

"He had an affair with Bev Carrigan. A *long* affair."

Trey said nothing.

Troy increased the speed on the windshield wipers. "Mom probably knew. Or found out."

Trey had heard enough. He'd only just been out a couple hours. He wasn't ready for family conflict and drama. "They're all gone now, and the past is the past. Maybe it's time to let sleeping dogs lie."

"Except they're not all gone, and it's not just the past." Troy flexed his hands against the steering wheel again. "Because there is something else going on—"

"Another affair?"

"No, but with Callan." Troy shot him a swift glance, brow creased. "When her dad passed, he didn't leave the place to her. Or any of them."

"*What?*"

"There's some talk in town—just gossip at this point— that maybe he wasn't their biological father—"

"Bullshit."

"Well, why didn't he leave the Carrigan ranch to his kids?"

"I don't know. But Callan must have been pretty broken up. She loves that place."

Troy was silent a moment. "I think Dillon knows something, too, but he's not saying."

"Those two friends again?"

"More friendly than friends. While you were gone they became drinking buddies. Every Friday night you can find them at Grey's, playing pool and shooting the shit." Troy's lips curved. "Dillon practically lives at Grey's on the weekends."

"He's not driving back to the ranch drunk, is he?"

"Usually he finds a warm bed in town, along with an even warmer woman."

"Our Dillon is a player."

"He's certainly enjoying being a bachelor."

"No little Sheenans on the way?"

"None that I've heard about." Troy leaned forward, turned up the music and then halfway through the Martina McBride Christmas song turned it back down. "There's something else I've got to tell you."

Trey glanced warily at his brother. "Brock got cancer?"

"Um, no. Thank God." He sighed. "But it's not going to make you happy."

Trey stiffened. "No?"

"It's McKenna."

Trey held his breath.

"I didn't know how to tell you, or when to tell you, but seeing as you're out today, now, you're going to need to know." Troy's eyes narrowed and his jaw tightened. "McKenna is getting married tomorrow."

They drove another mile in deafening silence, snow pelting the car and windshield. Trey stared out the window blindly, seeing nothing of the Tobacco Root Mountains and Three Forks before them. Instead he fought wave after wave of nausea. McKenna getting married....McKenna marrying tomorrow...

Unthinkable. Impossible.

His stomach rolled and heaved. He gave his head a sharp shake. This couldn't be happening. He couldn't lose her now, not after waiting four years to make things right.

"Hey, Troy. Pull over." Trey's deep voice dropped, cracked. "I'm going to be sick."

Chapter Two

THESE WEREN'T BUTTERFLIES McKenna was feeling. They were giant wildebeests swarming with flies. So no, she wasn't nervous. She was *terrified*.

Not terrified of marrying Lawrence, but terrified that if she didn't marry him, the rest of her life would be just as hard as it'd been the first thirty-three years.

She was ready to lose the Douglas off her name. Ready to no longer be that tragic McKenna Douglas who'd lost five of her immediate family members as a not-quite-fourteen year old in the Douglas Home Invasion Tragedy nineteen years ago. People spoke of it like that, in newspaper headlines.

She was ready to stop being the brave girl folks hovered over, worrying about, petting, protecting to the point that McKenna couldn't show fear or anxiety or everyone would hover more and worry more and suffocate her with the worrying that changed nothing, and the hovering that made it impossible to breathe. The only one who never hovered and worried was Trey and she'd loved him for it.

And hated him.

But that was neither here nor there. He was the past and today she was stepping into a bright new future as Mrs. McKenna Joplin, Lawrence Joplin's wife.

She was more than ready to relinquish the title of 'devoted single mom'. Of course she was devoted, she was a mother. And yes, like all moms, she tried to be a great mom, but she was ready for a partnership, ready for a daddy for her boy, and a warm, kind loving husband to help carry the burden…emotionally, physically, financially.

Lawrence would be a great partner, friend, and father for TJ, and just minutes from now she'd be walking down the aisle, joining Lawrence at the altar. But my God, the butterflies…

The wildebeests…

They were bad. She was shaking. She was this close to throwing up.

From joy, not nerves.

And okay, maybe a little bit of nerves and exhaustion thrown in there, too, as TJ had spent the last week sick with a virulent flu and she'd been up with him, night after night, fussing over his temperature, holding him as he heaved into the toilet, measuring out thimblefuls of fever reducer and pain killer since his five year old body ached and ached so that her normally busy and bright boy was a whimpering tangle of arms and legs against her.

She loved that boy to distraction. Some said she loved

him too much. But how could you ever love a child too much? Children needed love...tons and tons of love. And fortunately, TJ was better—bouncing back the way five year olds do—and at this very moment, tearing away with her brothers in the groom's dressing room. Even better, she hadn't come down sick, herself, so everything was good.

Everything was fantastic.

Which was why her eyes burned a bit, and her heart thudded. The only thing that could make today perfect was if her mom and dad could have been here, and Grace, Gordon, and Ty...

There were days where she didn't think about them, those who died at the house that day, and then there were days she couldn't forget them. Today was one of them. But then, it was natural for a bride to wish her mom was there to help her dress, and her dad was there to walk her down the aisle...

She blinked hard, quickly, holding back the emotion even as the door to St. Jame's bridal dressing room opened, and the delicate light bright strains of Vivaldi reached McKenna, the organist continuing to make her way through the prelude play list, and then the heavy oak door closed behind Paige Joffe, silencing the music.

"The church is full," Paige said, hands on her hips. "The flower girls are in place. The bouquets are in the foyer. All we need is you."

McKenna nodded and reached up to wipe beneath her

eyes to make sure they were dry. "I'm ready."

But Paige heard the wobble in McKenna's voice and was immediately at her side, ruby red bridesmaid dress swishing. "What's wrong, Kenna?"

McKenna shook her head, forcing a smile. "Nothing. Absolutely nothing!"

"You're sure?"

"Yes."

"You're not getting cold feet, are you?"

"No!" McKenna's voice rose, horrified. She didn't have cold feet. Her nerves weren't cold feet. Her nerves were an accumulation of emotion. Fear, hope, love, loss, longing.

But was there a bride who didn't feel emotional? Was it such a bad thing to be a tiny bit apprehensive? She wasn't a twenty-two year old virgin. She was a mother, and it'd been just her and TJ for years. Now she was moving her boy into a new home, another man's home. Thank goodness Lawrence wasn't like those testosterone driven alpha males who were all weird and territorial about raising another man's child. He wanted to be a good stepfather. He wanted to do scouting with TJ and teach him to fish and how to throw a ball.

Not that Lawrence could actually throw a football. Or catch a pop up ball. But her brothers could teach TJ those things. Her brothers were tough and testosterone-fueled. What TJ needed was Lawrence's quiet strength. His calm, his self-control.

So, no, Lawrence Joplin wasn't a he-man, cowboy, athlete, bar room brawler. But he was invested in the community, and constantly giving back, which made him the right example for TJ Sheenan. The right example for a little boy who was growing up with his biological dad in jail.

"You look beyond beautiful," Paige said, giving McKenna's silk train a shake to make sure it didn't wrinkle. "Simply gorgeous," she added, adjusting the long veil to float above the gleaming white silk.

McKenna looked at her reflection in the antechamber's oval mirror, thinking she'd taken so many photographs of brides in this very spot, doing one last make up check before leaving the dressing room for the church. It was a bit surreal being the bride herself today, and not the photographer. She was far more comfortable being in the background than in the starring role.

Paige kept up a steady stream of chatter to try to distract McKenna. "TJ looked adorable. I love tuxedos on little boys, so cute." Paige had been McKenna's best friend for the past two years, from practically the moment she arrived in Marietta with her two young children in tow.

"I hope he's behaving," McKenna answered.

Paige grinned. "He's trying his best."

McKenna smiled ruefully. "Are my brothers losing their minds?"

"Not too badly. And your brothers seem up for the challenge."

"I think they wish he had more Douglas in him and less Sheenan."

"But you love that little boy because he's all Sheenan." Paige leaned in and gave McKenna a warm hug. "Now don't be sad," she added, her voice dropping. "This is a happy day. You're marrying your best friend. Lawrence is as steady as a rock. You know he'll always be there to take care of you."

Paige was right. Lawrence was exactly that—steady and reliable. A tad conservative, too, but she'd learned the hard way that conservative was better than crazy-ass wild. "I just hope that he'll always be as patient with TJ as he is now, because a spirited five year old is one thing, but a sassy or sarcastic thirteen year old is another."

"You'll just have to work hard to make sure TJ doesn't get sassy or sarcastic—"

"If he's anything like his dad, he's not going to be a saint, and you to have admit, he's the spitting image of Trey."

"I haven't actually met Trey, but I know Troy, and yes, TJ is a miniature of his uncle Troy."

"If only he acted like Troy…instead he's wild. Wild like Trey."

"Wild and adorable," Paige retorted. "The cutest kindergarten kid ever, with an incredible sense of humor."

McKenna smiled a watery smile. "He does have a good sense of humor."

"Yes. He's hilarious. And he just needs a good kind father figure, a father who is there." Paige hesitated, picking her words carefully. "Is this about…Trey?"

"No!" McKenna shook her head. "*No.*"

"You're sure? Because it's not too late—"

"I'm sure." McKenna's voice hardened. "Absolutely sure. At least, with regards to him. He had his chance. He had dozens of chances. He's not an option. At all. In any way."

Paige reached for the box of tissues and pulled two soft sheets. "Look up," she said, before dabbing beneath McKenna's eyes. "I know you two had a stormy relationship, but he is TJ's dad."

"Then he should have acted like TJ's dad. He should have been careful. He should have been responsible. He should have put his family first."

The door to the dressing room opened, organ music swelled in the background, and Rory Douglas, McKenna's oldest brother, stuck his head inside the dressing room. "I think they're ready for you, Kenna," he said.

And just like that, the butterflies were back. McKenna placed a hand across her stomach, calming the flutter followed by a wave of nausea. Coffee with weak toast probably wasn't the breakfast of champions. "How's TJ?"

"Looking sharp." Rory crossed the floor, caught her in a quick hug. "And you, Kenna, you're one hell of a beautiful bride. Mom and Dad would be so proud of you."

And just like that, the tears were back, and the knot of hot emotion. She clung to her handsome big brother, fingers digging into his arms, needing the support. "I miss them," she whispered against his chest. "I miss them so much, Rory."

"I know, kiddo. I know." His voice dropped low, his tone husky. "But I'm sure they are here with us today. I'm sure they're looking down on you, as proud as anything."

"You think so?"

"Yeah, Kenna, I do." He stepped back and kissed her on her forehead. "Now no more tears. You don't want to mess up all that make up." He glanced at Paige who was picking up McKenna's heavy train. "Does this mean we're ready?"

McKenna smiled through her tears. "I think so."

"Then I'll round up TJ and meet you in the vestibule."

Chapter Three

TREY SAT IN his truck in front of Marietta's St. James Church watching the second hand on his watch, aware of every passing minute.

Two minutes after four o'clock.

Three minutes after four o'clock.

If the four o'clock candlelight wedding had started on time, McKenna would already be down the aisle, at the front of the church, getting ready to say I Do in front of Marietta's most respectable citizens.

It would be a beautiful ceremony. The bridesmaids would probably be wearing red. It was a Christmas wedding after all.

Four minutes after four o'clock.

If he was going to do this, it had to be now, before she'd said her vows.

He grimaced, aware that his appearance would be problematic. McKenna was not going to be happy to see him. No one was going to be pleased by his appearance...not even

Troy, who was sitting inside with his librarian girlfriend.

Common sense and decency forbad him from interrupting McKenna's wedding.

But Trey apparently had neither.

He glanced down at his watch. Five minutes after four o'clock.

If he was going to do this, he had to do it.

He drew a deep breath, feeling the snug blazer pull across his shoulders. The jacket was too tight. The trousers a little too fitted. It wasn't his suit. It was Troy's, and if the hand sewn label inside the jacket was any indication, very expensive.

He didn't have to dress up today. One didn't need to be in formal wear to interrupt a wedding, but he wanted to be respectful. This was McKenna's big day. So he'd borrowed his brother's suit, and paired it with a black dress shirt, but had passed on the tie—he wasn't a tie guy. He was wearing black boots with the suit because those were the only dress shoes he owned, but he did feel a bit like Johnny Cash, The Man in Black.

Today the black shirt wasn't a fashion statement.

Today he'd dressed for a funeral. McKenna marrying Lawrence was an end...the death of a dream. But he wasn't going into the church to fight, or to protest. He just wanted to speak to McKenna, to make sure she'd recognize his rights as TJ's father. Because he could maybe—just maybe—accept losing McKenna, but he couldn't wrap his head around losing TJ.

TJ was his boy. His son. His flesh and blood.

He loved that boy, too. Fiercely. Completely.

But that didn't matter in a court of law. Not when McKenna had sole custody, just as she'd had sole custody from the beginning, and let's face it, no judge would ever take him from his mother, not when the mother was as good as McKenna, and the father as rotten as Trey Sheenan. Or so said Judge McCorkle when he gave McKenna sole custody all those years ago.

Six minutes after four o'clock.

He hadn't slept last night. Couldn't sleep after failing to find McKenna earlier in the evening. And even though Troy and Dillon had warned him off, Trey had gone looking for her. He had to. He had to talk to her—not just about her choosing Lawrence, but about TJ, and what would happen to TJ once she married another man. So after showering and changing at the ranch house yesterday afternoon, he'd grabbed the keys to his truck—which still ran thanks to his brothers taking care of it—and headed back to Marietta to try to find McKenna.

He'd searched for her without success. She and TJ no longer lived in the old apartment complex, the one by the Catholic church. Part of him was glad—it was a crappy neighborhood—but he didn't know where they'd gone and the few folks he asked either didn't know or weren't about to tell him.

But she had to be somewhere. She was getting married the next afternoon, which meant there had to be a rehearsal dinner someplace that night in Marietta. Maybe at Beck's, or one of the other nice new restaurants that had opened in the last few years, or at the Graff, not that he could see any sign of McKenna or a wedding party there.

It was possible they were doing a BBQ dinner at one of the fancy barns, or even hosting the dinner in Livingston or Bozeman.

Trey had been sure Troy knew, and Dillon, too. But they weren't talking.

In the end, Trey had gone to bed at midnight and spent most of the night lying on his back staring up at the beamed ceiling of his bedroom, trying to imagine the future without McKenna and TJ, aware that he'd be lucky to see his son a couple days a month.

Trey, who had a cast iron stomach and nerves of steel, had thrown up again in the middle of the night.

If only he'd been able to talk to her.

If only he'd been able to have a chance to plead his case, asking her to consider joint custody, asking her to promise more visitation time...

She needed to know how much TJ meant to him.

He glanced out the window, up at the sky. The sun was dropping, shifting, soon to disappear behind the mountains, leaving Marietta in darkness. He looked from the sky to his watch. Eight minutes after four.

If he didn't do something soon, it'd be too late.

If he hoped to state his case, it had to be now.

But he dreaded what was to come. He dreaded making her unhappy. She wouldn't appreciate him interrupting the wedding, creating drama. Even he could see the pattern there. Trey = Chaos. Trey = Shame.

But he wasn't doing this because he wanted to embarrass her. He was doing what he had to do to protect his rights as a father, even if he was only allowed to be that father on a part-time basis.

It was now or never. And God help him, but he couldn't handle forever without his boy, so it looked like the time was now.

Trey shook down his sleeve, covering the watch, and opened the truck door.

Things were going to get interesting fast.

MCKENNA STOOD AT the back of the church, trembling in her high heels, praying no one knew she was about to wobble her way to the altar. This was supposed to be a slow and stately procession down the aisle, but she didn't feel stately at the moment, not with her legs shaking and her knees knocking.

It was the blasted Wedding March that made her shake. Those loud, bright chords so familiar to all. The entire congregation had risen to their feet at the first one, heads swiveling to the back, one hundred and fifty pairs of eyes fixing on her.

She'd smiled to hide her terror.

She wasn't an exhibitionist. She'd never liked being the center of attention. This was definitely a lot of attention.

Rory covered her fingers where they rested in the crook of his arm and gave an encouraging squeeze. "Buck up," he said with his deep, low-pitched voice. "You got this."

She flashed him a smile, a real smile, some of her tension easing. "This is crazy," she whispered. "So many people."

"All here for you, darlin'."

And then they were walking, and she wobbled in her heels, but not as badly as she'd feared. She pulled her shoulders back with every step, standing taller, her attention on Lawrence and TJ where they stood together at the front of the church.

TJ was wriggling away from Lawrence, trying to escape.

Lawrence's hand rested on TJ's shoulder, trying to keep him in place.

In a flash, McKenna saw the future, realizing that this was how it'd always be. They were so different, those two. TJ would always pull one way and Lawrence would pull the other. She'd have to be careful not to get caught in the middle. She'd have to learn to be neutral so that she didn't put herself in the middle.

And then she was there, with Lawrence and TJ and all the groomsmen before the altar, the dark wood pews filled with family and friends behind her.

The music died.

The priest spoke a few words and Rory placed her hand into Lawrence's and stepped away.

Rory stepping away was significant. She was leaving the Douglas family to start a new life as a Joplin. Her chest squeezed with a rush of emotion. Her life was changing. Everything was changing. She was glad. But it was also somewhat overwhelming—

"Wait. Stop." A deep voice rang out from the back of the church. "I'd like a word with McKenna."

She knew that voice.

But he couldn't be here. He couldn't be. He was in jail.

Wasn't he?

Heart thudding, she pulled her hand from Lawrence's to turn around, aware that the church had gone strangely quiet. No music. No voices. Nothing but Trey in the middle of the red carpeted aisle, and candles flickering on the lip of each of the stained glass windows.

Dark handsome Trey, still so tall and lean and intimidating even in an expensive black suit and black dress shirt.

For a moment she couldn't breathe. For a moment she just looked at him, gaze locking with his.

Trey.

Here.

Now.

For a moment all she could do was drink him in as the past fell away and the future disappeared and there was nothing but now. And he looked more beautiful now than ever before. Her beautiful Trey.

Her beautiful destructive Trey.

He'd had this effect on her from the very beginning...such a fierce, visceral reaction. A recognition so deep that she couldn't remember a time when he hadn't felt devastatingly important. Just one look into his eyes and she felt connected, connected deep, all the way through her heart and tissue and bones.

No one had ever understood her love, or attraction. Friends had rolled their eyes when she said she felt connected to his soul...

It wasn't normal, they said. Wasn't healthy.

But that was how it had always been with them.

Deep and fierce...a love that was all consuming. A love that was endless.

"Momma." TJ was suddenly there at her side, his small fingers snaking into her left hand as she clutched her bouquet in the right. "Is that...is that—"

"Hello, Tiger." Trey's deep voice seemed to rumble from his chest. The corners of his mouth lifted but his expression looked pained.

Haunted.

"Daddy?" TJ whispered.

McKenna's eyes burned. Her pulse continued to race. "This isn't the time, Trey," she said quietly, and yet in the hush of the church, her voice carried, clear, loud.

"If you'll excuse us—"

"I need five minutes."

Rory was on his feet. "You don't have five minutes."

Quinn rose, tall and broad, next to Rory. "Think you need to see yourself out, Sheenan."

Trey didn't even glance at her brothers. His gaze rested squarely on McKenna and TJ. "Five minutes," he repeated.

"I don't want this to be ugly," Rory said, leaving the pew, moving towards McKenna.

She lifted a hand to stop him. She had to control this. Her brothers would just make it worse. "TJ's waited a long time to see you," she said, voice husky. "Protect him now."

Trey winced and glanced down at TJ, a shadow crossing his features. She saw pain in his eyes, regret, too, and she had to steel herself against the wave of emotion slamming into her, because Trey had made a lot of mistakes in his life but he had always adored his baby boy. He had always been so patient and sweet with TJ.

"Can we just step out and speak for a moment?" Trey asked, looking back up at her, looking straight into her eyes.

She started to shake her head. She started to tell him no but she could feel his anguish and his love for TJ, and it made her eyes burn and her throat swell closed.

She should hate him for what he'd put them through, but she couldn't hate him. Couldn't hate him when her little boy looked just like him, and walked like him, and talked like him. TJ was Trey in miniature...

She glanced at Lawrence, who'd come from the front of the church to stand behind her, somber and protective. "I'll be back in just a minute," she said crisply, before squaring her shoulders and marching back down the aisle, head high, refusing to make eye contact with any of the guests who'd been breathlessly observing the drama unfolding.

OUTSIDE AS MCKENNA faced him, Trey could tell she was fighting mad, her green eyes flashing, her high cheekbones a vivid pink.

She'd always been beautiful, but with her dark red hair swept up and covered by the tiara and veil, leaving her neck and shoulders bare, she looked ethereal and fragile, almost too delicate for the white silk wedding gown with the fitted bodice and full tulle skirt.

"You're thin," he said, frowning at her.

"I've always been," she retorted, shivering at a gust of icy wind. "And what are you doing here? I'd think this would be the last place you'd want to be."

He peeled his suit jacket off and moved to drape it around her shoulders but she took a swift step back. "No, thank you," she said shortly.

"It's thirty one degrees. I can't have you freezing."

"I won't be out here long enough to freeze." Her chin lifted. She stared him down. "Why are you here? What do you want?"

"You," he said bluntly.

"Too late."

"And my son."

"I've never kept him from you."

"Not true. You stopped bringing him to see me, and wouldn't let my brothers bring him for a visit."

"The prison visits were giving him nightmares."

"Seeing me scared him?"

"Leaving you each visit destroyed him." Her lips pressed thin. Her eyes shone emerald, the black mascara on her lashes wet. "He needed to be protected. He needed to be a child….innocent, free, happy."

"And so you stopped coming."

"I gave TJ his childhood back."

Her gaze locked with his, fierce and defiant, and as much as he hated what she was saying, he respected her position. "You should have told me that," he said. "At least I would have known what was happening and why."

Her shoulders hunched against another gust of icy wind. "I asked your brothers to explain."

He glanced up at the darkening sky. There were no clouds, and no snow in the forecast. "My brothers know better than to get involved when it comes to you and me." He thrust his jacket at her again. "Please put it on."

"I have to go inside. Lawrence is waiting."

"And TJ? TJ is still my son?"

"Of course he's your son."

"And you'll let him come see me on weekends…stay

with me on the ranch?"

"Well, eventually, maybe—I mean—he's just five, Trey."

"I know. I've missed out on four of his five years. I don't want to miss anymore—" he broke off as the church doors crashed open and TJ bolted outside.

"Mom! Momma!" he cried, racing towards McKenna with Lawrence hot on his heels.

"Stop, TJ," Lawrence said sharply, racing after the boy. "Stop! TJ, listen to me."

But TJ wasn't listening and he didn't stop until he'd flung himself against McKenna, his arms wrapping tight around her waist. "I wanted to see Dad," he said, pressing his face to her tummy. "But Lawrence wouldn't let me."

"Come back inside with me, TJ," Lawrence said, putting his hands on TJ's shoulders. "It's cold out here and your mother needs to talk."

TJ shrugged a shoulder, shaking the hand off. "She's talking to my daddy."

Lawrence's jaw tightened in exasperation. "Come inside, son."

TJ squirmed away, glancing shyly at Trey. "I want my daddy. My real daddy. *Him.*"

Chapter Four

TJ's innocent words made McKenna go hot then
cold. Lawrence must be beside himself. She was beside
herself. Nothing was going today as she'd expected.

"I'm sorry," she said to Lawrence.

He just shook his head, uncomfortable, and probably
offended.

She swallowed hard, confused and conflicted. She should
reprimand TJ for being rude to Lawrence, but how could she
get angry with TJ when he was staring up at Trey in shock
and awe?

"Give us a minute, hon," she said softly to Lawrence,
reaching out to take his hand. She gave his cold fingers a
squeeze, hoping he wouldn't feel rejected. "Let TJ have a
minute with his dad."

But Lawrence wasn't in a mood to be placated. He was
annoyed, embarrassed, and yes, deeply offended. "His *dad?*"
he echoed, angry and surprised. "Since when has Trey
Sheenan acted like a dad? Since when—"

"*Lawrence*," she choked on his name, cutting him short, squeezing his hand again, expression pleading. She couldn't do this now, couldn't fight with Lawrence, not on their wedding day. But she also had to be sensitive to TJ's feelings, and for that matter, she wouldn't shame Trey in front of his son. "I know this is hard, but let me handle this. It won't take long. I promise."

Lawrence pulled his hand from hers. "Everybody is wondering what's going on out here. Everyone is worried about you, McKenna."

"They don't need to be worried. Everything's fine," she answered.

"If everything was fine, you'd be in the church, McKenna, not out here with your—" Lawrence shot Trey a caustic glance, "*ex.*"

The doors of the church swung open again. "You okay, honey?" Aunt Karen called to her.

McKenna looked up and Aunt Karen, Rory, Quinn, Paige, and Troy Sheenan had all crowded into the doorway. Paige looked anxious, Aunt Karen indignant, Troy troubled, and her brothers ticked off.

"I'm fine," she answered, checking her irritation. "We're almost through here and I just need everyone to go back inside and let me finish speaking with Trey—"

"And leave you alone with that convict?" Aunt Karen demanded. "I don't think so!"

Trey shot McKenna's aunt an incredulous look. "You

think I'd hurt my girl?"

Lawrence stiffened. "She's not your girl anymore, Mr. *Sheenan*. She's my wife—"

"Not yet your wife," Trey corrected, "still just a bride."

"If you'd let us finish the ceremony, she'd be my wife."

Trey's dark head dipped, conceding the point. "True."

Aunt Karen wagged her finger at Trey. "Why aren't you in jail?"

"Got out early," Trey answered, smiling faintly. "Good behavior."

"Hah!" Karen snorted. "Don't believe that for a second. You probably broke out. They're probably looking for you now."

His lips curved higher. "With guns and dogs."

"I knew it!"

"It's good to see you, too, Karen."

"Ha!"

Lawrence shifted his weight, arms folding across his chest. "Karen's right. What do you want?"

Trey's smile faded. "Nothing from you."

"Then perhaps you'd be kind enough to go? As you might have noticed, we're getting married today, and it's a day we've looked forward to for a very long time."

"I respect that, sir, I do," Trey answered. "And it looks like a lovely wedding. The candlelit church is a very nice touch. But I've waited two years to see my boy, and I'd like just a few minutes with his mother to sort out our son's future."

"Sorry to be the bearer of bad news, but nobody's going to be able to sort out TJ's future today." Lawrence managed an apologetic shrug. "And certainly not now, in this court-yard, when we have guests waiting inside."

"I hate to inconvenience your guests," Trey retorted. "But if I could just speak to McKenna without the aunts and brothers and onlookers, we could be done in just a few minutes."

Lawrence turned red. "And what's so important that it has to interrupt *my* wedding? This is *my* wedding, *sir*. I think you forget yourself."

Trey didn't move, but McKenna felt him tense, energy shifting, muscles coiling. "This isn't about me, Larry, this is about my son, and I'm sorry you've got to cool your heels, wait five minutes for my girl to become your wife, but I need to know he's going to be okay—"

"Okay? TJ has it made. He's going to have the best of everything with me—"

"But he won't have me," Trey shot back.

Lawrence looked smug. "Exactly."

"No more," McKenna choked, stepping between them, arms extended, a referee in the ring. "I can't do this. I won't do this. Not today." She looked at Lawrence, tears in her eyes. "Don't provoke him," she whispered. "Please don't make this worse than it is." Then she looked to Trey. "And you, stop throwing your weight around. You've been gone four years. You don't get to waltz in and demand your parental rights. If those rights were so important to you, you wouldn't have thrown us away in the first place!"

Both men stared at her, expressions grim.

"You are not dogs," she added, "and TJ is not a bone. Respect me, if you can't respect each other!"

Lawrence stepped close to mutter, "It's only difficult because you're letting him be difficult, McKenna."

She lifted a brow. "He's TJ's dad."

"Only in name. You and I both know he's never tried to act like a father—"

"I'm not going to argue about this now. And I refuse to embarrass TJ, or Trey. This isn't the time."

"But you'll embarrass me?"

"No!" She winced at the gust of frigid air, goose bumps peppering her arms. "I thought you of all people would understand how important this moment is for TJ, and how important it is that we protect his feelings—"

"He should know the truth about his dad. He should know Sheenan is no good, and has a criminal record a mile long—"

"That's not true. The only time he's ever been in trouble was for fighting," she protested through chattering teeth. She was cold all the way through. "Now, I'm freezing, and I'm sure you're freezing and we both would love to be inside and getting married. So let me send Trey on his way, and you go tell our guests that I'm coming, and we'll still have our wedding day, okay?"

Seconds ticked by. Lawrence ground his teeth together, then shook his head. "I don't like this."

"I know. I don't either. But he'll be gone soon and everything will be fine. I promise."

Lawrence stalked off, and ushered the gawkers in the doorway back inside.

McKenna waited for the tall wooden doors to close before turning to Trey, who'd wrapped TJ in his suit jacket.

"Your timing sucks," she said bluntly.

His broad shoulders shifted. "I tried to find you last night. I didn't want to do this today."

"When did you get out?"

"Yesterday."

For a moment there was just silence, and the cold air whistling through the valley. McKenna was so chilled now she wasn't sure she'd ever feel warm again. "Who told you?"

"Troy. Just before we reached Marietta." He exhaled. "I wished you'd told me. A letter...just a few lines..."

She said nothing. He was right. It would have been the right thing to tell him. The decent thing. But her relationship with Trey wasn't easy. Her feelings weren't simple, nor easily managed, at least, not when it came to him. The only way she'd been able to move on was to do it full stop. Cold turkey.

It'd hurt like hell. She'd suffered, especially as each of his frantic letters arrived, but she'd reached the end of her rope.

She had nothing left. Not for him, or them. She barely could keep it together for TJ, and that was the only thing that kept her from falling apart completely.

TJ needed one whole, healthy, available parent.

He needed her to be the whole, healthy, available parent. He depended on her for everything.

And so she stopped reading Trey's letters. She took down Trey's photos. She boxed up his extra jackets and boots and things he'd left at the apartment and dropped them off at the Graff Hotel, leaving them for Troy to deal with.

And gradually TJ stopped asked about his dad. They stopped discussing Trey. There was no mention of a dad, or a dad in prison. It was almost as if Trey had never been in the picture.

But seeing TJ and Trey together in the courtyard, McKenna knew she'd gotten it all wrong. TJ hadn't forgotten his father. It might have been two years since he last saw his dad, but TJ knew exactly who he was, and where he'd been, and from the wondrous look in his blue eyes, it wasn't going to be easy peeling TJ out of Trey's arms."

"TJ, honey," she said. "We need to go back inside. We still have the wedding and the party after—"

"Is Dad coming?" TJ asked hopefully.

"No, honey."

"Why not?"

"Because he's not...invited." Her stomach felt heavy, as if she'd swallowed a rock.

TJ wrapped his arm around Trey's neck. "Can I invite him?"

"No, babe. But you'll see him again…" Her voice faded. She struggled to smile, her eyes hot and gritty. It hurt to look at TJ and Trey together. "Soon."

"When?"

She blinked, clearing her vision. "After Christmas, after we get back from Disney World."

"Can Daddy come?"

"No."

"Why not?"

"It's…a honeymoon."

"But—"

"TJ, no." Her voice cracked. "Now say goodbye and don't be sad, because you'll see your dad in early January."

"Your mom's right," Trey said gruffly, putting TJ down. "No need to be sad. I'll be here when you get back."

TJ clung to Trey's fingers. "How long will you be here?"

"Forever," Trey answered.

TJ frowned. "You're not going back to jail?"

"No."

"What about the dogs? Will they get you?"

Trey crouched down and stared TJ in the eyes. "That was a joke. Your great aunt Karen was being funny. There are no dogs. No one is coming to get me." He clapped his hand on TJ's shoulder. "I'm home, son. For good."

"You're going to live with us?"

"With you and Mom and Lawrence? No, bud. I'll be at the ranch. Grandpa's ranch. You know, where Uncle Dillon lives."

"TJ doesn't go out there much," McKenna said quietly, uncomfortably.

Trey glanced at her for a split second, expression inscrutable, before returning his attention to TJ. "You'll live with your mom and Lawrence, but you'll see me. Evenings and weekends…whenever we can work it out."

TJ frowned. "But why do we have to live with Lawrence if you're not in jail anymore?"

"Because your mom loves Lawrence."

"But you're my dad."

"Yes, and I'll still be your dad, even when—" Trey broke off, took a deep breath, finishing, "—they're married."

"I don't know why they have to be married if you're here."

Trey clasped TJ's face in his hands and pressed a swift kiss to his forehead. "When you're grown up, you'll understand." He stood, and looked at McKenna. "I'm going to want to see him, Mac," he said roughly, using his nickname for her. "I need you to promise me that you won't keep us apart."

"I'd never do that."

"Or let Lawrence keep TJ away," he added.

"He wouldn't do that, either."

Trey's laugh was low and mocking. "I don't believe that

for a second, and neither should you. I want a promise. A cross your heart promise."

A cross your heart promise. That was the promise they used to make to each other...

Cross my heart, I promise to always love you...

Cross my heart, I promise to one day marry you...

Cross my heart, we'll raise our baby together...

She swallowed hard. "I promise. Cross my heart."

He nodded, apparently satisfied. "Now go inside before the two of you freeze to death." And then he was off, walking to his truck at the curb, his black dress shirt billowing from an icy blast of wind.

TREY WAS HALFWAY down the front steps when TJ let out a shriek and came running after him, his shoes ringing on the pavement. "Daddy, wait! Wait!"

"Stop, TJ!" McKenna's voice rose, short, sharp, firm.

"Daddy, don't go!"

Trey kept walking. He couldn't stop. Couldn't turn around. Couldn't look at his son or see his face, or those bright blue eyes. Couldn't let himself remember how good it felt to hold TJ in his arms, his son safe warm and good and still so very innocent.

TJ's innocence mattered. He was just a little boy. He deserved good things, and good people. He deserved to be protected. Which was why Trey had worried all these years, worried that while he was in prison McKenna and TJ were vulnerable. He'd worried about their safety, and their financial security. He'd worried that without him there to protect them, something horrible might happen, just as it had happened on the Douglas ranch when McKenna was just a thirrteen year old girl.

Trey shuddered at the curb's edge, his heart and mind in conflict.

McKenna needed Trey to walk away now. But did TJ?

Would leaving now be the right thing for his son?

He hesitated on the curb, hearing TJ's fast light steps behind him. The boy was running, his breathing ragged.

It tore at him, wounding him.

His boy running after him, wanting him, and he just leaving…

"TJ!" McKenna shouted again, louder, more frantic.

Teeth grinding tight, Trey stepped off the curb and into the street. He had to honor McKenna's wishes. He had to respect her. He had to be a man of integrity—

"*Dad!*"

TJ's panicked scream filled the air as Trey opened the truck door and climbed inside the cab even as he wondered how did a man live like this? Survive a life like this? He felt cursed. Broken. He loved McKenna and TJ but it didn't matter. He'd screwed up. Messed up. And he was always going to pay…

"Daddy!" TJ's voice rose higher. "*Wait! Wait for me!*"

Trey had just put the keys in the ignition but now he

froze, shoulders hunching.

Wait.

Wait for me.

But that was all Trey had done, the past four years. Wait, and wait, and wait.

The pain roared through him, hot, blistering. This was hell....pure hell...

And then suddenly TJ was there, climbing into the truck, his arms wrapping around Trey's neck.

"Don't go," TJ begged, voice trembling, "not without me."

Prison was bad, Trey thought, heart on fire, but this was so much worse.

This...there were no words for this...

Trey held TJ tight, breathing in his son's warmth and sweetness, aware that TJ belonged with his mom. By law, TJ belonged to his mom. There was nothing he could do at this point. Nothing he could do but reassure TJ that he loved him, and would always love him. "I can't take you now, son," he murmured, "but one day it'll be different. One day we will be together and do fun stuff together. Hiking and fishing and camping. Sports, too—"

"Not one day. Now," TJ said, arms squeezing tighter.

"I can't," Trey said.

"Why not?" TJ pulled his head back to look at Trey.

McKenna was there now, in the street, shivering, teeth chattering. "TJ, get out of the truck right now. I've tried to be patient. I've tried to be understanding, but I can't do it anymore. You can't do this now. We have everybody waiting. Lawrence is waiting—"

"I don't care!" TJ shouted at her. "I don't like Lawrence. I don't want Lawrence. I want my dad. He's my real dad."

McKenna paled. Her gaze lifted. She stared into Trey's eyes. "Trey, tell him he has to come with me. Make him listen to you. I'm sure he'll listen to you. Tell him he has no choice."

McKenna's eyes were a brilliant green, shimmering with emotion. She was angry and scared and he understood, he did. But at the same time, she had no idea what he'd been through, living without TJ these past four years. She had no idea what it was like to love someone so much and then be completely cut out...

Trey held her gaze, his voice soft. "Why doesn't he have a choice?"

Her lips quivered. She pressed down, thinning them. "He's five. He doesn't know what's true, or right, or real—"

Trey's brows flattened. "Real? Am I not real? Is my love not real? Am I not here, fighting for him, fighting for a chance to be his father?"

"That's not what I mean!"

"What do you mean?"

"He just...He just..." she took a quick breath, shivered, arms crossing over her chest, "doesn't *know*."

"Know what?"

She shrugged helplessly. "*You*."

"Then maybe it's time he does."

Chapter Five

MCKENNA SUPPRESSED A shiver as Trey's dark head jerked up, his narrowed gaze locking with hers. For a split second she could see his shock. She'd hurt him. But in the next moment, the surprise disappeared, replaced by fury.

Mistake, she thought, inhaling sharply, she'd make a big mistake. Perhaps even a critical error.

You didn't really want to make Trey angry. Not truly angry.

When pushed too far, Trey didn't bend or yield. He didn't compromise, nor was he a man of words.

Trey Sheenan was a man of action, and she could see from his hard, shuttered gaze that he was done talking. Done playing nice. Trey had tried diplomacy and he was reverting to what he did best: taking control.

Fighting.

And this time he was fighting her.

McKenna's heart pounded. Her legs shook. She took a step toward him. "No, Trey, no," she choked, seeing him place TJ in the middle of the truck's bench seat. "Don't do this."

He clicked the seatbelt around the child's waist and then turned the key in the ignition. The big truck roared to life. He had to raise his voice to be heard over the powerful engine. "I won't have him thinking I don't love him, Mac. I won't have him believing I don't care—"

"But this isn't the way, Trey. This isn't the answer."

His brow creased, his jaw thickening. "He thinks I don't love him. He thinks I don't want him. Nothing could be further from the truth."

"Take him out of the truck."

"And put him on the curb and drive away like he isn't my whole world? Like he's not the most important thing in my life?" He drew a swift, shallow breath. "TJ's the only reason I survived in that place. He's the only reason I'm still here." His deep voice dropped as he spit the words at her, each syllable sharp and rough. "He's five and I've only had one Christmas with him and I want more. I want more with my son. And I deserve at least one Christmas with him before he becomes part of your new family with this other man."

"TJ will always be your son, Trey."

"Then you shouldn't mind him spending one Christmas with me." He slammed his door closed and shifted gears.

She pounded on his door. "You're not taking him! You're not—" She broke off as he swung the door back open. She fell back a step, tripping over the hem of her gown. "You can't, Trey. It's wrong. It's illegal. You'll be charged with kidnapping!"

"I've been charged with worse," he retorted grimly.

She shook her head frantically. "But not this, Trey."

"I don't want my son to grow up without me."

"You can't just take him from me."

"Fine. Then you can come with us, too." And with stunning ease, he stood up, picked her off the ground and dropped her onto the truck seat, next to TJ. "Buckle up, darlin'. We're heading out of town."

TREY HAD DONE a lot of stupid things in his life, but this might just be the stupidest.

But had no choice. He had to do something. He couldn't just stay there on Church Street fighting with McKenna in front of TJ and St. James.

She wasn't fighting fair. Women never fought fair. They argued. They yelled. They cried. They used torrents of words, endless words, words that drowned a man in sound and nonsensical emotion.

He'd tossed her into the truck because he wanted TJ, and he knew very well he couldn't take TJ from his mom, not on Christmas.

What kind of man would he be to separate a mother and young child on Christmas?

So he was bringing her along. Letting her come. He was being generous and thoughtful.

Magnanimous.

Not that she'd see it that way.

Nor would her groom, who they'd just left in the church with the guests and her brothers and his brother and good old Aunt Karen...

Aunt Karen would be the one to call the sheriffs. Aunt Karen would be delighted to hear he'd been arrested. *Again.*

Something hard and sharp turned in his gut. Regret filled him.

He'd just screwed up badly, hadn't he? She sat beside him, a blur of white in his peripheral vision and didn't say a word, but he didn't need her to. He knew it. He knew what he'd done.

He flipped on the truck lights as he approached Highway 89, steering with a tight knuckled grip that made his hands ache. It was dark out. The wind whistled and howled.

He fiddled with the truck heater, the truck interior almost as chilly as the frigid temperature outside. But the biting cold was nothing compared to the ice in his heart.

He'd made a terrible mistake just now.

What was he thinking? Taking TJ, and McKenna, too?

What kind of madness had taken over him back there at St. James?

Merging onto the highway, easing into the traffic, he kept his gaze fixed on the road, while McKenna's silence felt as huge as her gown.

He'd thought he'd finally grown up. He'd thought he'd changed. He was wrong. He was still stupid and impulsive, and what he was doing now, heading north on 89 with TJ and McKenna, was illegal. McKenna was right. This *was* kidnapping.

He'd only been out of jail one day and he'd already broken the conditions of his parole.

Trey exhaled in a low, slow rush, sickened, aware that he'd just proven Judge McCorkle and Karen Welsh and all the other skeptics that they were correct: he was a loser. A bad seed.

Leopards didn't change their spots.

It didn't matter now that he'd left Deer Lodge determined to make amends and be the stand up father TJ deserved. Good intentions were just that—intentions. What mattered was actions. And just look at his actions...

McKenna's stillness only made his regret worse.

He glanced at her from the corner of his eye. She was rigid, staring out the window, her expression one of shock. And horror.

He'd failed her, *again*. Ruined one of the most important days in her life.

Damn all.

But TJ was oblivious to the tension. He'd buckled his seatbelt as they'd pulled away from the curb and now he was sitting tall, trying to see over the dash, curious about where they were going, but not afraid. From his bright eyes he looked excited. This to him was a great adventure.

McKenna must have her hands full with him. TJ didn't

just look like a Sheenan, he seemed to have inherited the Trey-Sheenan-Chaos DNA.

Not good. For McKenna, Marietta, or TJ himself.

Trey struggled to think of something he could say to her. He wanted to apologize, and yet at the same time he knew that if he was truly sorry, he'd turn around right now and take her back. Take them both back.

Taking them back now, before they traveled any further, would at least allow her to salvage today…marry and have her party and cake and dancing.

But he wasn't that sorry.

He didn't want her to marry Lawrence. He understood why she wanted to get married, why she wanted stability, but Lawrence…? *Really?*

McKenna deserved a real man. A strong man who'd love her deeply, passionately for all of his life.

The way he loved her.

The way he'd always love her.

He glanced at her again, the deepening twilight swallowing her profile. "McKenna—"

"Don't say it."

"I'm—"

"You're not. And I don't believe it. I know you." Her voice was hoarse and it shook, trembling with emotion. "I once thought you were a dream, but I was wrong. You're not a dream. You're a nightmare, a never ending nightmare—" She broke off, shook her head, turned her face away, her white veil gleaming in the lavender-purple light.

He winced.

He deserved it, though.

"An Enderman," TJ said brightly, breaking the silence. "You're an Enderman, Dad."

Trey glanced at him. "A what?"

"An Enderman," TJ repeated. "An evil guy from Mine Craft. He's all black kind of, like you."

"What's Mine Craft?"

"My favorite game. But I can only play on the weekends when I don't have school and Mom lets me use her iPad."

"Is there a good guy in Mine Craft?"

"Yeah, Steve. But I like Endermen better. They're crazy. They're also called Henchmen and they kill things—" he broke off, looked at Trey. "Not real things. It's just a game. I promise."

Trey wasn't sure he liked being compared to a bad guy, and was pretty certain the comparison wasn't lost on McKenna, either.

MCKENNA DIDN'T KNOW if she should laugh or cry. Only TJ would think it was cool that his dad was a bad guy.

A henchman.

Only TJ would love an Enderman over Steve, the Mine Craft protagonist.

Only TJ would enjoy the drama and be excited about a road trip with his man-in-black, bad guy father.

But she wasn't TJ. She wasn't a wild, reckless Sheenan. She was a Douglas. She tried hard to be good, and thought-ful. *Kind.*

And yet, being kind today ruined everything.

At the church, she'd wanted to be kind and protect Trey's feelings. She'd tried to save him from being embar-rassed in front of his son. What a tactical error that had been, because in trying to protect Trey's feelings, she'd lost control of the situation, giving Trey the upper hand.

And he hadn't worried about her feelings. He hadn't worried about doing the good thing, the kind thing. No, he'd swooped in, and taken advantage of the upper hand. He'd exploited her weakness.

But then, when had Trey had ever tried to be kind?

She bit down into her lower lip, trying to hold in all the angry words, not wanting to escalate things further, not wanting to get hysterical when TJ was caught in the middle.

TJ.

She glanced down at him and he was smiling, blissfully oblivious to the angry currents, or maybe being a Sheenan, he just didn't mind them. Maybe being a Sheenan, he enjoyed the tension and fighting.

It boggled her mind that her son, the child she'd raised single handedly for the past four years, was his father in miniature.

How was that right?

How was that fair?

But then of course, life wasn't fair. She'd learned that in 8th grade when she'd kissed her family goodbye and hopped into seventeen year old Rory's truck so he could drive her to Jessica's for a sleep over.

Her parents and three youngest siblings were slain within a half hour of her leaving. Fifteen year old Quinn—the only one at the house who survived—had been bludgeoned like the others, and left to die.

Quinn wasn't supposed to survive. It was a miracle he had. But that night changed everything. That night taught her that life was short, and fate was capricious, and there was only now. There was only the present. You couldn't go back. You couldn't live in the future. Instead there was today, and today was too important to waste with anger, hatred, or regret.

Far better to live fully. Far better to love completely. Far better to forgive and forget and count one's blessings.

This was the philosophy that had allowed her to love Trey all these years.

Forgiving, forgetting. Counting one's blessings.

But after fifteen years of forgiving and forgetting she was tapped out. Her patience and her emotional reserves were gone. She had nothing left to give Trey. Nothing left at all, she repeated, watching the purple sky darken until the truck's head beams were just pale circles of light piercing the night.

Unable to bite her tongue a moment longer, McKenna

blurted, "This is crazy, Trey."

He didn't even hesitate. "Yeah."

She heard the disappointment in his voice and it made her ache, and the fact that she could still care about his feelings just made her angrier.

She shouldn't care for him. She shouldn't care at all. He deserved what he got. He did.

He did.

She swallowed hard, fighting the lump in her throat. "So what *are* you doing?"

This time he took a moment to answer. His big shoulders shifted. "Buying time to be with my son."

"Wrong way to go about it."

He laughed low, the sound mocking. "When have I ever gone about anything the right way?"

"It's one thing at eighteen, Trey, another at thirty-something!"

"Yeah. I know." He shot her a swift glance, his profile hard in the dim light of the dash. "On the bright side, at least I'm giving you the chance to reconsider your decisions, and maybe you'll come to your senses and realize that Lawrence isn't the right guy—"

"And you are?"

"No. Not saying that. Couldn't say that, especially not now, after doing this, but there has to be someone else in Marietta for you. Marrying Lawrence would be a mistake, and you know it."

"Falling in love with you was the mistake!"

"Probably, so let me do you a favor. Help you out before you compound your mistakes. You don't want Lawrence. He won't make you happy. You and TJ both deserve better."

"How can you say that? You don't even know him!"

"I might not win any debate competitions, but I'm a pretty good judge of character."

"Huh!"

"And Lawrence is weak. He has no back bone."

"You think he should have wrestled you to the ground?"

"I think he needs to be a better role model for TJ."

"*What?*" She shot TJ a swift glance and saw from his expression he was listening. She dropped her voice, trying to sound less agitated and confrontational. "He's a perfect role model for TJ. He doesn't drink or speed or stay out late or fight—"

"He probably pays all his taxes on time, too."

"Yes, he does. And he donates money to lots of local charities."

"What a great guy. Next thing you'll tell me he volunteers to serve up meals at a homeless shelter on Thanksgiving morning."

"He has in Bozeman, yes."

"Wow, Mac. You lucked out. Larry Boy's a real Prince Charming."

"Yes. He is. And his name is Lawrence, not Larry, so knock off the attitude, turn this truck around now, and take us back. I love him—"

"*Please.*"

"You're so childish."

"I'm not saying you need to love me, but honestly Mac, he's too soft for you. And TJ will run all over him. Lawrence won't have a clue how to manage our son."

She looked away, staring pointedly out the window, even as his words ate at her, making her feel raw.

Trey was saying all the things she secretly worried about. Could Lawrence handle TJ? And maybe Lawrence could manage TJ now, but what about when TJ was ten? Thirteen? Seventeen?

What then?

But she wouldn't let Trey know she was afraid, wouldn't give him the satisfaction.

Instead she had to get through to him. She had to talk sense into him, make him understand that this—what he was doing—was going to backfire in a horrible way.

"Just take us back," she said, voice low. "It's not too late to turn the truck around and take us back. I won't press charges. I just want—"

"*No.*" Trey's hands tightened on the steering wheel, his broad knuckles shining white against his olive skin. "No," he repeated more quietly. "I can't. I want a chance to get to know my son first."

"Just because I'm getting married doesn't mean you're losing your son—"

"That's not true. You have custody. Full custody—"

"You weren't around for shared custody, buddy."

"I get that. But I also know how this will work. You marry Larry and TJ will live with you and Larry, and Larry will become the Dad. I'll be that guy who sends lame gifts on birthdays and Christmas."

"Then don't send lame gifts."

Trey shot her a narrowed glance. "In the old days I would have laughed."

"Yeah. 'Cause in the old days it would have been funny." Her throat ached and her eyes burned. "But this isn't funny, Trey. What you are doing isn't funny. It's illegal. You're breaking the law. You'll be going back to jail for a long *long* time—"

"Yeah, I pretty much figured that out."

"So turn around!" she begged, heartsick.

"Darlin', I'm already screwed. Everybody in that church knows what happened. I've no doubt in my mind that Larry or one of your brothers has alerted the police. It's not a question of if I'm going back to prison, it's just a matter of when. So, since I'm going back behind bars for another couple of years, I want a Christmas to remember. A Christmas when we were almost a happy family."

"*Trey.*"

"I understand you don't love me. I won't ask you to love me. But I will ask you to let me be my son's dad for a few days. That's all I want."

She looked at him for a long minute, taking in his hard beautiful profile, a profile that glowed in the light of the dash.

He was bad....he was trouble...and yet whenever she'd needed him, he'd been there. When she'd been terrified of the dark, scared of the bad buys, scared that she'd be attacked and murdered, he'd held her and protected her, vowing to keep her safe.

And he didn't just do things like that for her. When Neve Shepherd had disappeared in the river after the 1996 prom, he and Troy had driven their pickup back and forth along the river bank with Trey at the wheel, shining their headlights in the water for an hour, trying to find her. Trey had driven with huge skill. He hadn't wanted to give up. He'd hated that neither he nor anyone else had managed to save her.

As long as he lived, he'd promised McKenna, no one would hurt her.

As long as he lived, he'd vowed over and over, she'd be fine.

And she'd believed him.

She'd felt so safe with him...

McKenna turned her head away and stared out the window again, unable to see anything through the hot tears blurring her vision.

She'd once loved him so much. He'd been her everything.

McKenna blinked back the tears. "I hate you," she whispered. "I hate you, Trey Sheenan."

He was silent a long moment and then he sighed. "As you should."

Chapter Six

THEY DROVE THROUGH Livingston, and continued north for nearly another hour, the highway a dark ribbon beneath the rising moon. TJ broke the silence to ask if he could play a game on McKenna's phone.

"I don't have my phone, TJ," she answered.

"It's not in your purse?"

"I don't have my purse." She shot Trey a glance. "I don't have anything but what I'm wearing."

TJ was silent a moment, processing, and then he looked at Trey. "Do you have games on your phone?" he asked hopefully.

Trey grimaced. "I don't have a phone."

TJ's brow creased. "*Here?*"

"At all." He looked down at TJ. "You can't have one where I was."

"Ah." TJ pursed his lips and thought about this for a few seconds. "But you're out now. Don't you want one?"

"Yes. I just haven't had time to get one."

"Didn't you have one from before?"

"I did. But it's old now. Technology changed while I was away."

TJ nodded. "There's a new iPhone out now, you know. Mom wouldn't get it though. She said her old one still works. But I'd like one—"

"How do you know all this?"

"Commercials. TV." TJ shrugged nonchalantly. "And from Mom and Lawrence talking. He wanted to get Mom a new phone but she said no."

Trey glanced down at TJ again. "Are all five year olds as smart as you?"

TJ thought about it a minute then shrugged. "Some. Some aren't." He thought about it some more. "Lawrence thinks I'm too smart. He says I'm going to end up just like you."

McKenna winced, even as Trey exhaled hard.

That couldn't have felt good to hear, she thought. But what did he expect? He'd never been Marietta's model citizen, but going to prison and leaving her alone with a baby certainly hadn't endeared him to the community.

"I hope you don't end up like me," Trey said after a long pause, his voice pitched low and heavy. "I want you to be better. I want you to be successful. Be a good man. Be strong and smart. Do good in school. Be the man your mother is raising you to be. Make her proud, TJ. Make her happy."

FOR THE NEXT thirty minutes no one said much of anything, but after a while, TJ got restless and he shifted on the seat, drawing his legs up and then down, leaning first against McKenna and then on Trey.

"I'm hungry," he said grumpily. "And I have to go to the bathroom."

"Me, too," McKenna agreed, thinking that if they stopped she could use a phone and call Lawrence and let him know what was happening. She didn't want him calling the sheriff or the police. The last thing TJ needed was to see his father arrested in front of him.

"We are almost to White Sulphur Springs," Trey said. "There's a little diner just a mile or so from here. Nothing fancy, but food's warm and the floor's clean."

"Do they have chicken?" TJ asked.

"Yes," Trey answered.

"And buttered noodles?"

"I'm sure they do."

"Good. Let's go there."

The diner's parking lot was empty except for a couple of pick ups and a lone big rig parked in a far corner of the lot.

A few evergreens hugged the broken asphalt, and years of snow and ice and heavy trucks had pitted the parking lot's surface.

Climbing from the truck, McKenna's heels caught in the cracks and ruts, making her stumble.

Trey scooped up TJ who was still wearing Trey's suit

coat, and came to her side. "TJ, what if we give your mom the coat? She's not wearing much and it's cold out."

"No, thank you, I'm fine," she answered crisply. "Let's just get inside. It'll be warm there."

"So stubborn," he muttered, putting his hand at her elbow to help guide her across the icy parking lot, but she wasn't having that, either, and tugged her arm free.

"I'm not an old lady, Trey. I can manage."

But this time he ignored her, and took her arm again. "It's dark and slippery and you're wearing high heels and right now I don't feel like rushing you to a hospital should you fall and break something."

"I'm not going to fall and break something!"

"And I'm not going to argue." His fingers closed around her elbow. "Let's just get inside."

In the diner bathroom, a shivering McKenna shut the stall door behind TJ and turned around to face the mirror. She blinked when she caught sight of her reflection.

Oh.

Oh. *Wow.*

She knew she was in white, knew she'd been driving for an hour and a half in her dress and pearls and veil with the sparkling tiara. But she'd forgotten the impact of so much white, had forgotten she looked so very…bridal.

TJ emerged from the bathroom stall, struggling to close the zipper on the little black trousers that matched his tuxedo jacket. "Can't get it," he said, frowning.

"Let me," she answered, crouching in front of him, and fastening the snap at the waist band and then pulling the fabric taut and away from him, not wanting to catch his boxers or boy parts in the zipper. She'd done that once, when he was two. She'd never forget it, either, and ever since always zipped him up oh so carefully. "There. All boy junk safe and sound."

TJ grinned, a lopsided grin that was so Trey it made her heart ache. "You're crazy, Mom."

"I know." She chucked him gently under the chin and stood up. "Wash your hands while I use the restroom. Use plenty of soap and water, okay?"

"Okay."

In the narrow stall it took some maneuvering to get the full skirt and tulle petticoats up, and the silky fabric and train out of the toilet, but she managed without damaging the dress too much, although the hem was dirty in places, probably from the walk across the parking lot caked with packed dirty snow and salted ice.

She'd woken up feeling emotional this morning. She'd felt jittery at the church, and worried about everything going well, but it had never crossed her mind, that this was how today would go...

Practically kidnapped at the altar by Trey.

TJ was waiting for her by the sink, his brow wrinkled and expression brooding.

"What's wrong?" she asked him. "You okay?"

"*No.*"

"Want to talk about it?"

"Lawrence said after you marry him I have to call him Dad. But I don't want to. He's not my dad."

"He's going to be your step-dad. That means you're lucky. You get two dads—"

"He's not my dad," he stubbornly repeated.

"I think you're being a little mean to him because your real dad's home, but that's not fair to Lawrence who has always been really good to you."

"Because he likes you."

"Lawrence likes you, too."

"Not that much."

"Oh, TJ, that's not true. He cares a lot about you!"

"Then why does he smile weird when he talks to me? Like he's got to poop and doesn't want anyone to know it."

"Trey James!"

"It's true."

"You are being ridiculous!" She turned to the paper towel dispenser and took a paper towel to dry her hands. "And rude." She shot him a disapproving glance. "I won't tolerate you being rude to him, either. He hasn't done anything to deserve disrespect." She held his gaze. "You know what disrespect means, don't you?"

He hung his head. "Yes."

"You're to be polite, and kind. You're to listen and follow the rules. Understand?"

He hung his head lower. "Yes."

She threw away the towel. "Now let's go have dinner and I'm going to call Lawrence and Aunt Karen and let everyone know we're fine. Lawrence will come for us and we'll go back to Marietta and tomorrow everything will be normal again."

She started for the door but TJ hung back. McKenna glanced over her shoulder. He was still standing there, small and dejected. She suppressed a sigh. What was the matter now? "TJ?"

He looked up at her, worried. "Are they going to arrest him? The police? Are they going to take my dad?"

Her chest squeezed. She felt a flutter of panic. "I don't know—" she broke off, grimaced. "Maybe."

His eyes filled with tears. "Will they handcuff him, like they do on TV?"

Her heart fell. "I hope not."

"'Cause he's bad?"

A lump filled her throat. Her eyes felt gritty. "He's not *bad*...not really."

"I heard you say that he's going back to jail and he'll be there forever."

Of course TJ was listening to everything. TJ was her little silent sponge. "I don't know what's going to happen to your daddy, but let's not talk this way. It makes me sad."

"But you hate him. I heard you say that in the truck. Two times."

"I shouldn't have said it. It wasn't nice of me. It wasn't kind."

"But you do hate him."

"TJ, he's your daddy. He loves you a lot. And we're here right now because he loves you so much, so let's go have dinner with him and not worry so much, okay?"

He stared at her a long time, expression brooding.

"TJ?" she prompted.

"I just don't understand," he said.

"Understand what?"

"If he loves me so much, why do you hate him?"

"It's complicated." She hesitated. "And I don't hate him."

"Then why did you say it? It was mean. It hurt his feelings."

They exited the bathroom to find Trey was waiting for them by the hostess stand, a red flannel shirt bundled under his arm. "I remembered I had this tucked behind the seat. It's been sitting there for a long time, but it should keep you warm." Trey gave the large cherry red flannel shirt a shake, and held it out to her.

She opened her mouth to say she was fine, but she wasn't fine. She was cold and tired and sad, worried about Lawrence and TJ and how everything had changed so fast that she couldn't get her head around it.

Right now she should be at the wedding reception at the Graff, finishing dinner, or perhaps having the first dance.

Instead she was here, at a rustic diner outside White Sulphur Springs, a town with a population of less than a thousand.

She was definitely over dressed and over exposed for a Montana diner that was pretty much in the middle of nowhere.

"I'll take the shirt, even if dusty." She slipped the soft flannel over her shoulders, pushing her arms through the sleeves, buttoning the front and tying the long shirt tails around her waist to keep her warmer. And she was warmer, and she did feel better. "Thank you."

"By the way," Trey said, "there is only one waitress on tonight and the regular cook didn't show so service will be slow and the meal questionable."

"Do you want to go somewhere else?" she asked.

"I was wondering about that."

"I just want to eat now," TJ said. "I'm hungry."

McKenna glanced around the mostly empty restaurant. Just a half dozen tables were filled. It couldn't be that much of a wait here. And then she spotted the phone by the cash register. She could call from that. As soon as they ordered, she'd ask if she could borrow it. Lawrence and her family must be frantic. She didn't want them sending out search parties. "Let's just stay."

The waitress, an older woman in a red checked apron, emerged from the kitchen's swinging doors, flushed but smiling. "Sorry to keep you waiting. A bit hectic in the kitchen but everything is good. Homestyle cooking at its finest."

McKenna smiled. "Sounds great."

"And it looks like congratulations are in order," the waitress added. "We don't get many wedding parties here. You all look so nice." But she frowned for a moment at the ill-fitting red flannel shirt. Reaching for menus from the hostess stand, she chucked TJ under the chin. "Especially you, little fellow. You look very sharp."

"My mom was going to marry Lawrence but then my dad came so now we're here."

"Sounds like a great day," she answered, obviously not understanding anything TJ was saying.

McKenna managed a faint, weak smile. "It's certainly been a day of surprises."

The waitress grinned back. "Aren't those the best kind?"

TREY TOOK A seat on one side of the burgundy booth tucked along the wall, and McKenna and TJ sat on the other. Trey barely glanced at the plastic coated menu but TJ wanted to have all his options read to him, even though McKenna knew he'd order chicken and buttered noodles.

The waitress returned a few minutes later with glasses of water and to take their order. Trey wanted a steak sandwich and TJ chose his chicken and buttered noodles. McKenna was more stressed than hungry and asked about the diner's soup.

"It's vegetable beef," the waitress answered. "It's from

yesterday but it's good. I had some earlier."

"I'll have a cup of that," McKenna said, closing her menu. "And coffee, please."

The waitress put away her notepad. "Cream with that?"

"No, thank you."

"Is the coffee fresh?" Trey asked.

"Brewing a new pot now."

"I'll have a cup, too," he said.

"Two coffees coming up," the waitress said. "And what about the little guy? Milk, chocolate milk, juice?"

"Milk," McKenna answered. "Thank you."

The waitress headed to the kitchen and McKenna glanced to the register and phone. She needed to call. She should do it soon.

As if reading her mind, Trey said, "You need to call. Everybody's going to be worried."

McKenna nodded. "Yeah."

"I'm sure the waitress will let you."

McKenna nodded again. She was dreading the call. It wouldn't be easy. Nothing about this was easy.

Trey was studying her face. "What's wrong?"

She shrugged. "It's going to get messy. Fast."

"It's already messy," he answered.

"Yeah, but—" she broke off as the waitress returned with their coffees and the milk for TJ.

"Anything else?" the waitress asked.

"Would it be all right to use the phone?" Trey asked.

"It's a call to Marietta."

"Sure thing, hon. You know where the phone is? On the counter, up front? Help yourself. Just dial normally."

"Thanks."

The waitress moved on and McKenna looked at Trey. "You didn't have to do that. I could have handled it myself."

"Just trying to help you."

"Mr. Helpful, that's you."

His blue eyes sparked, lips curving slightly. "I can be good."

"Mmm."

"I was instrumental in making Deer Lodge's ranch program successful."

"You've always been a good rancher. That was never the problem."

"I always loved you, and TJ."

"Your love wasn't the problem, either." She sipped her coffee. It was surprisingly strong and hot. She sipped again. "I think you know what the problem was."

"You've always known who I am. I've never hidden it from you."

"It's one thing to fight at seventeen, and another when you're a thirty-one year old man with a fiancée and a baby."

"Who did you kill?" TJ blurted.

"Who told you he killed someone?" McKenna demanded.

"Lawrence." TJ shrugged. "He said he wasn't supposed

to say anything, and so I shouldn't say anything to you 'cause it'd upset you." He looked across the table at Trey. "Did you really kill someone?"

"Yes," Trey said bluntly. "I did. I didn't mean to kill him though. We got into a fight in a bar."

TJ clasped his milk, more intrigued than scared. "How you'd do it?"

Trey held his gaze. "I punched him."

"You punched him to *death*?"

"No. I hit him three times. On the third punch he went backward, hit his head on the edge of a table. He died a couple of days later."

"The police arrested you?"

Trey nodded. "There was a trial, and two days before your first birthday I was sentenced to five years in jail."

"What's jail like?"

"Bad. You don't want to ever go there."

"I used to go there. That's what Mom said."

"Yeah, but it's not a place for kids. It's not a place you want to visit again." Trey looked up at McKenna. "I didn't know why you stopped coming to see me, but I do now. And you were right. It wasn't the place for him." He hesitated. "Or you."

McKenna struggled to speak around the lump in her throat. "I should have explained it to you. I should have told you—" she broke off and bit down into her lip. "It's been such a mess, hasn't it?"

Trey grimaced. "Still is."

"Yeah." She glanced toward the phone, knowing she needed to make the call, knowing that the moment she made the call everything would change. Again.

"What are you worried about?" Trey asked, still able to read her so well.

Aware that TJ was listening intently, she picked her words with care. "I'm concerned Lawrence will have made some calls."

"I'm sure he has," Trey said bluntly. "If the situation was reversed, I would have."

"I don't think more…messy…is good for…anyone." She glanced at TJ who was toying with his milk glass but his dark head was bent, and she knew he was taking it all in. "And I definitely don't think it's good for him."

TJ glanced up, and looked from her to Trey before returning his attention to the glass.

"So what do you want to do?" Trey asked her, leaning against the burgundy vinyl, by all appearances comfortable and relaxed. But appearances were deceptive. This was Trey's best defensive position. He was always relaxed before a fight.

She clasped her coffee mug between her hands, warming them. "Avoid unnecessary drama."

"How do we do that?"

She shot TJ another quick glance. "We have dinner. You go. I call. We wait for Lawrence to come."

"I just leave you here?"

TJ's shoulders hunched up. Her own insides churned. It took her a moment to reply. "I don't know who will show up. I don't know how all the pieces will come together. I do think it'll be less—tense—if it's just me and TJ here."

Trey's jaw tightened. He looked away, out the front window onto the dark, mostly empty parking lot.

He didn't like the plan. He was wrestling with himself. It wasn't his nature to walk away from those he loved. If left to him, he'd rather stay and get handcuffed and hauled away, than to drive away, leaving them behind.

She nearly reached out to touch him but remembered herself at the last second. "I know you don't want to," she said quietly, fingers curling into her palm. "But it's better. Better for him."

Trey glanced at TJ, and TJ looked up at that moment, to meet Trey's gaze.

Two Sheenans, cut from the very same fabric.

Her jaw ached and her eyes burned. She wished she could protect them both, but that was impossible. So she had to do the next best thing, protect their relationship. They loved each other. They needed each other. And they hadn't had enough time with each other.

"I'll go home and smooth things over," she added. "We'll let things settled down and then with a little luck and maybe some finessing, we can get you two together for Christmas, for a bit—"

"What is a bit? An hour? Two?" He shook his head.

"That's not Christmas."

"It's better than the alternative."

"But is this the future? That I'll have to learn to be grateful for an hour with my son on Christmas?"

"I hope not."

"Me, too."

They both watched TJ who was frowning into his milk, his forehead furrowed.

Trey shifted then abruptly said, "I'll leave as soon as we're done eating."

She nodded, grateful. "Will you head to the Sheenan ranch?"

"I don't know. Depends on how things work out."

"I'm not pressing charges. Nobody will come after you—"

"That's not the point. I just can't be there without you and TJ. There's nothing for me in Marietta if I don't have you."

"You've got your family—"

"*You* and TJ are my family. You're the ones I love. Without you, there's no point in sticking around—"

"Can I go wash my hands?" TJ asked, interrupting, showing them his palms. "They're sticky."

"I'll take you," McKenna said, sliding out from the bench.

"I can do it myself," TJ answered, climbing from the booth. "I'm in Kindergarten now."

She smiled a little. "Okay, but hurry. Dinner will be here soon."

Chapter Seven

T REY WATCHED MCKENNA'S gaze follow TJ across the
diner, her expression troubled.

"You're a good mom," Trey said quietly. "He's so lucky
to have you."

She looked at him, tears in her eyes. "He's missed you.
So much."

"He's a sweet little boy. Smart, too."

"You're smart. Very smart. You just never liked following
the rules."

"True."

"TJ doesn't, either."

"That could be problematic."

"It already is." She struggled to smile. "I worry about
him. I worry that no one will understand him. I worry that
people will judge him...much the way they've judged you."
Her voice broke and she looked away, swiftly wiping tears
from beneath her eyes.

"It's going to be okay, Mac."

She looked at him, eyes wet. "Will it?" she asked hopefully.

Her make up had begun to fade and her high cheekbones jutted, her skin pale, gleaming like porcelain.

She looked younger without the blush and lipstick. More like his McKenna, the one he'd met his senior year at Marietta High when she was just a wide-eyed freshman, and the baby sister to Rory and Quinn.

It was impossible not to notice McKenna when school started in September. She was on the Frosh-Soph cheer squad and wore the short uniform red and white skirts every Friday, game day, and with her long bare legs and dark red hair spilling all the way down her back, she looked like a siren, and yet she was only fifteen years old.

He did his best to avoid her. He didn't want to be attracted to her. He didn't date freshman. He didn't even like dating sophomores. But every now and then he'd find her looking at him, and she looked at him in a way no one else ever did.

She looked at him as if she could see him, see who he was, not who he pretended to be.

She looked at him as if he was good. Maybe even wonderful.

It made him feel funny, and his chest would get heavy and tight, and he became protective of her, not just because she was that Douglas girl, and not because she was impossibly pretty, but because she made him believe that maybe he was worth something. That maybe even though he was brash and reckless and in and out of trouble, that there was something still decent in him. Something real that had value.

And so he went out of his way to avoid her, not wanting to be tempted, because he was already far too tempted.

He stopped glancing her way when he knew she was around. He refused to meet her gaze. He wouldn't get to know her.

He didn't want to disappoint her, and it was inevitable he'd let her down. In his eighteen years, he'd disappointed everybody else.

But McKenna didn't take the hint. She didn't go away. She shadowed him as they took the same path to their respective fourth period classes. She stared at him as he hung out with the other seniors during lunch. She'd stand with her books on the sidewalk bordering the school parking lot waiting for her ride, and yet he sensed she wasn't as much waiting to be picked up, as waiting to watch him walk by.

From all accounts she was a nice girl, and a smart girl, taking honors courses and getting straight A's.

Why was she so interested in him?

He'd thought initially it might be the good girl-bad boy opposites attract thing, but she wasn't one of those sheltered good girls. She wasn't naïve. A year or so earlier she'd had her world blown wide open with the horrific home invasion on the Douglas Ranch and she was still coming to terms with the unthinkable tragedy.

You'd think she'd want to stay away from trouble.

You'd think she'd feel safer with the nice guys that hit the Honor Roll.

She was the one that approached him between classes, the day before the two week Christmas break. She was selling Christmas ornaments—flat brass angels—as part of a choir fundraiser and she wondered if he wanted to buy one.

Or several.

She was happy to sell him a dozen.

It was for a good cause.

He'd watched her face while she talked, fascinated by the curve of her lips and the glint of laughter in her wide, cat eyes. She was pretty at a distance, but stunning up close, her face all elegant lines and planes—cheekbone, jaw, nose, lips. But it was her eyes, jade green with flecks of sapphire and gold, that made it impossible to look away.

So he didn't.

He cornered her against the gym wall and stared into her eyes. "And what would I do with a dozen angels, little girl?" he asked, his voice low, husky. Dangerous.

He saw the flicker in her eyes and the tip of her tongue dart to wet her upper lip. He couldn't tell if she was afraid or intrigued.

"Give them as gifts," she answered coolly. "Your mother and girlfriend might like one."

"I don't have a girlfriend."

"Well, your mother."

"So that's one. What about the other eleven?"

"You could hang them in your truck, put them in your room, string a few over your bed." Her long black lashes blinked, her expression innocent. "Might help keep you out of trouble."

She knew his reputation, then.

And she wasn't afraid.

"I see you watching me," he said.

"How is that possible?" she asked, arching a brow. "You never look at me."

He looked from the winged brow to the full curve of her lips. His body hardened. Damn, she was hot.

And she was also fifteen. Only fifteen.

"How much are the ornaments?" he asked gruffly.

"Fifteen each, or two for twenty-five."

"And if I buy twelve?"

"I'll buy the popcorn when you take me to the movies this weekend." She smiled up at him, eyes dancing. "There are lots of really good movies out right now, and I'm free Friday and Saturday—"

"I'm not a big movie guy."

"Then we can skip the movie, and just go park."

She hadn't really just said that, had she? For a split second he couldn't breathe. "You're *fifteen*," he said, voice strangled.

"I'm not asking to have your baby."

"Good. Because you're not going to have my baby." He

stared at her, baffled, fascinated, outraged. And wildly turned on. "You're out of control."

"I'm not, actually. I don't mess around. I've never even been kissed." She took a quick breath, her smile unsteady, her confidence flagging. "But I'd like to kiss you."

"McKenna Douglas," he growled.

"So you do know who I am."

"Of course I know who you are. I know which classes you have. I know what you eat for lunch. And I could probably tell you what you wore every day this week."

Her lips parted, then closed. Pink stormed her cheeks. "Really?" she squeaked.

And it was that breathy little squeak that did him in.

She was gorgeous and sweet and smart and far too good for him. But he needed her. He needed someone good like McKenna to believe him in.

He bought the brass angels, a whole dozen, and he gave one to his mother for Christmas and hung the other eleven from his truck, his room, the mirror in the bathroom, and yes, on fishing wire over his bed.

Trey shifted in the diner booth and looked past McKenna's shoulder towards the bathroom. "Maybe I should check on him."

He rose without waiting for her to respond.

MCKENNA SAGGED AS Trey left the booth, his long strides carrying him across the diner floor.

For the past two years she'd known that TJ was looking more and more like his father, but she'd forgotten the details. She'd forgotten the way Trey made a room feel small and other people boring. She'd forgotten Trey's height and his sheer physicality. He was stronger than other men, more charismatic, too. But his nearness was wreaking havoc on her nerves. She felt tangled up in emotions she didn't want, and couldn't handle.

For two years she'd worked to forget him.

For two years she'd pretended he didn't exist.

But he did exist. He was here. And already he was changing everything.

Trey wasn't gone long. In fact, he seemed to walk into the men's bathroom and out again. He opened the women's door, stuck his head inside and then he was walking back to the table. "He's not there," Trey said bluntly.

She was on her feet. "*What?*"

He peeled money from his wallet and dropped the bills on the table. "We've got to go find him."

CARS AND TRUCKS whizzed by on the highway, headlights blindingly bright. The sky was clear and the moon shone white, no clouds to diminish the brightness. McKenna was grateful for the moonlight as she and Trey traveled the perimeter of the parking lot, searching for TJ, calling his name.

She was shivering from the cold, her tulle and silk skirts

tangling between her legs, but there was no way she'd go inside until TJ was found.

Cupping her hands to her mouth, she shouted his name, telling herself not to panic, telling herself he was here somewhere. He hadn't been gone long. There was no way he could have gone far.

Trey reached for her hand, taking it in the dark. "We'll find him, Mac."

His fingers curled around hers, his hand warm and hard, the skin callused on his palm.

She felt Trey's heat as his fingers laced with hers. His touch was meant to be comforting and yet she felt only electricity, as if he'd plugged her into something live and potent.

Just like it used to be.

But no, it wasn't like it used to be. It'd never be that way again.

"I think I see him," Trey said, releasing her hand and taking off at a run, darting across the highway to the other side of the road.

She watched him duck behind a cluster of garbage cans and come up with a little boy.

TJ.

Her heart lurched with relief. Thank God. Trey had found him.

Chapter Eight

INSIDE THE DINER, Trey put TJ down and McKenna didn't know if she should hug her son or shake him.

"What were you thinking?" she cried, crouching in front of TJ, holding him by the upper arms. "You could have been hurt out there, or killed! Why on earth would you do something like that?"

"I'm running away," he said hotly, totally unrepentant.

"Why?"

"'Cause you're making Dad go, and so I'm going, too—"

"I'm not making your dad go—"

"Yes, you are. I heard you. You said that he had to go so Lawrence can come get us and take us home, but I don't want to go with Lawrence. I don't like him. I'm not going to live with him."

"Oh, TJ—"

"I'm going with my dad," he interrupted fiercely. "You can go live with Lawrence."

"What about me? Won't you miss me?"

"No!"

"No? Why not?"

"Because you're sending him to jail!"

"I'm not."

"I heard you." His pressed his mouth shut in a mutinous line for a moment. "And if you send him to jail, I'm going with him, too."

Her heart fell and she sank back on her heels, full white skirts puffing around her like an airy cloud of meringue. "Oh, honey."

"I will," he insisted, arms crossing defiantly over his chest. "Where he goes, I go."

"They don't send little kids to jail." She folded her hands in her lap, studying his unhappy face. "Not even if they're bad. And you're not bad." She glanced past TJ to Trey who stood with his arms folded, too. Like father, like son. "Neither of you are bad," she said, holding Trey's gaze. "Sheenans aren't bad. A little hot-headed, yes, but bad….no."

TJ was still struggling to process everything. "So he didn't kidnap us?"

She leaned forward to kiss TJ's chilled cheek. "No, babe."

"And he's not in trouble."

"No."

"So he doesn't have to leave. He can stay with us and we can have Christmas together. Right?"

She struggled to smile. "How about we start with dinner

first? And then we can talk about Christmas after."

WHILE TREY AND TJ finished their dinner, McKenna used the diner phone to call Lawrence.

He didn't pick up on his cell. She hung up without leaving a message and tried Paige, who didn't answer, either. McKenna wondered where everyone was, and what they were doing. She prayed no one was out searching for her and TJ.

Prayed that everyone was calm and pragmatic. But if she wanted everyone calm, then she needed to let people know what was going on. How could she do that, though, when even she didn't know what was happening?

"Hey Paige, it's McKenna," she said, getting Paige's voice mail. "I'm with TJ and Trey and we're fine. I'm calling from a restaurant phone, where we're having dinner. Trey and TJ are eating and talking and doing some bonding. Please tell everyone that we're all good and no one needs to worry. We'll be back soon and I'll explain everything then. Could you please let my brothers and Aunt Karen know I called? Love you. Bye,"

McKenna hung up, and taking a breath for courage, she dialed Lawrence's number again.

She really needed him to answer. She really needed to tell him what was happening. But once more she went to his voice mail, and this time she didn't hang up but listened to his entire greeting, which was very lengthy as he gave his office hours and address, but then the beep sounded and she had to speak.

"Hi, Lawrence, it's me. It's about six thirty or seven I think, and I'm outside White Sulphur Springs, calling from the restaurant phone. TJ and I are fine. I'm so sorry about this afternoon. . ." Her voice trailed off and for a moment she didn't know what to say.

It was ending, wasn't it?

She couldn't imagine how she and Lawrence would ever recover from this. And suddenly she wasn't sure she wanted them to recover.

Trey and Lawrence would never see eye to eye and she couldn't bear for TJ to grow up, caught in the middle. And he would be caught in the middle.

She'd be trapped, too.

McKenna tugged on the phone cord and drew a quick breath. "I won't be back for a few days, probably not until Christmas. TJ and Trey have really missed each other and need to spend some time together. I want them to have this time. You've always said TJ was too much like Trey, and now that I see them together, you're right. They are alike and they need each other...they need a chance to be a family together..."

Her voice trailed off as she struggled to think of a way to end the call. "I hate doing this over the phone. Hate doing this in a message, but I don't want you wondering and worrying about us so I just want you to know that we're okay, and safe. I hope you're okay, too."

"And I'm sorry," she added softly. "I'm sorry for disappointing you, but we're not the right family for you. We're not the ones who will make you happy. There's someone else for you, I'm sure of it. I hope one day you'll understand and hopefully forgive me."

She gently set the receiver down, ending the call.

For a long moment she just stared at the phone.

She'd just ended it with Lawrence. It was over. They were done.

Chapter Nine

FROM THEIR TABLE at the diner, Trey could see McKenna on the phone, but he couldn't hear what she was saying. She dialed three different times, and each call was short. From the brevity of the calls he suspected she was leaving messages. It'd be interesting to know who she'd called and what those messages were.

TJ's voice caught his attention. "What's that, son?"

"Why didn't you apologize?" TJ repeated. "If you didn't mean to kill that man. Why didn't you say it was an accident and you were sorry?"

Trey glanced from McKenna, who was heading back to their table, to TJ. "It doesn't work that way," he answered. "An apology doesn't change some things."

"But you didn't want to kill him."

"No."

"Did you want to hurt him?"

"No."

"What did you want to do then?"

He hesitated. "I wanted him to stop hurting someone else."

TJ put his fork down. "Who was he hurting?"

"We shouldn't talk about this."

"Why?"

"It's just going to upset your mom—"

"What will upset me?" McKenna asked, sitting down at the table and placing her crumpled veil on the seat between her and TJ.

Several long dark red tendrils had come loose from the elaborate twist at the back to frame her face. Trey wished she'd take the pins out of her hair and let it spill free. She had the most gorgeous hair. He couldn't understand why she'd ever put it up.

"Talking about the man he killed," TJ said bluntly. "He said it makes you sad if we talk about it around you."

"He's right." She looked baffled. "Why are we discussing this again?"

"TJ wanted to know why I didn't apologize, since it was an accident," Trey tried to sound just as matter of fact but he hated the subject. It was obviously a sensitive subject. Trey had spent a lot of time at Deer Lodge asking himself what he would do differently, if he had to do it over again. Ignore Bradley beating up his girlfriend? Walk out of the Wolf Den as if nothing bad was taking place?

Trey couldn't.

He'd never be able to stand by as a man used a woman as

a punching bag. He'd never be able to allow a person to hurt an animal. He'd never let anyone abuse or threaten a kid.

It wasn't his nature. It wasn't acceptable to his own code of conduct.

Sure, when he was younger, he fought to fight. He'd liked fighting. He hadn't been afraid of taking a hit, either, because he realized physical pain was temporary. The real pain was the abuse that went on behind closed doors, the suffering of women in bad marriages, the agony of children raised by unstable parents.

Trey's dad had never hit his mom, but he didn't love her, and she'd suffered. She'd been a beautiful young woman when she married Bill Sheenan—and she'd given him five sons, one after the other, but his affections were elsewhere, with Bev Carrigan, and his mother had known.

She'd taken her life the summer after he and Troy had graduated from high school. Troy had been the one to find her. Their family had never been the same.

How could it be without their mother?

"None of it should have happened," Trey said flatly. "It's a day I will regret for the rest of my life."

"But why did you hit him?" TJ persisted.

Trey opened his mouth but no sound came out. How could he explain to a five year old that he'd seen a man using his girlfriend as a punching bag, so he'd intervened. The man, seriously inebriated, threw a punch at Trey, and Trey answered. A fight ensued and then Bradley lost his balance and went down.

If anyone else had stepped in that day, the outcome would have been different. Even the judge said as much. There might not have been an arrest, and there certainly wouldn't have been a five year prison sentence, but it was Trey Sheenan who'd interfered, and Trey had a long history of fighting in Crawford County, and Judge McCorkle wanted to make a point that he wouldn't tolerate thugs and petty criminals while he was on the bench.

McKenna sat forward. "Your dad went to jail because he tried to save a woman who was getting beat up by her boyfriend. Your dad didn't think it was right so he stepped in and there was a fight. Your dad is really strong, and a really good fighter, and he threw a hard punch which made the other guy fall, and when he fell he hit his head, and later died." She exhaled, face pale. "He didn't mean for the other man to die. It was an accident, and he did apologize to the family, but it didn't matter. Someone had died."

TJ frowned. "But a man should not hit a woman."

"That's right," she agreed.

"So my dad's a good guy? A hero?"

She made a soft, inarticulate sound as she glanced at Trey. "I guess it depends on who you talk to."

Trey held her gaze a long moment before fishing out his wallet and peeling two twenties from the other bills and leaving them on the table. "Should we go?"

They left the diner and crossed the parking lot quickly to

climb into Trey's truck to escape the cold. He started the truck and turned on the heater but it'd be a while before it put out hot air, and McKenna wrapped her arms around TJ to keep them warm.

He glanced at the shivering pair. It was damn cold. None of them had proper clothing for a Montana winter night. "What now?"

"What do you mean, what now?" McKenna answered, her gaze lifting to his, her winged eyebrows arching higher. "I thought you were the man with a plan. I thought you were determined to spend this Christmas with your son."

Her expression was mocking. She was throwing it down, daring him, challenging him, just as she had all those years ago when she was an innocent freshman and he the big bad high school senior.

Heat swept through him, blood surging through his veins, making him hot, and hard, filling him with longing for the life he'd had. The life he'd lost.

He missed her. He missed her body and her mind, her curves, her lips, her fire, her sweetness and that flash in her eyes. She knew him so well.

"That hasn't changed," he said, his voice low and husky.

"Then give TJ a special Christmas. Give him a Christmas he'll never forget."

TREY DIDN'T TELL her where they were going. He just drove and she was fine relinquishing control and being the passenger, settling in while he took them wherever it was he wanted to take them.

As they headed west on Highway 12, she'd wondered if they were stopping in Helena, but he kept going, passing through Helena, and then north on 83. They'd been driving for three hours and TJ had crashed out a couple hours ago, leaning against McKenna.

It was getting late and they were traveling a mountain road but McKenna was relaxed. Trey was an exceptional driver and he might make her nervous in a bar, but he was good behind the wheel, and his truck was a four wheel drive vehicle with snow tires so if they hit snow or ice they'd be fine.

And she felt fine, now.

Mellow. Thoughtful. A little sad, but not heartbroken.

That told her something, didn't it?

Shouldn't she feel a *little* devastated?

Shouldn't she feel something besides…relieved?

"Cold?" Trey asked, glancing at her.

She shook her head, and wrapped her arm more securely around TJ's hip.

They drove another five minutes in silence.

She could tell Trey had something on his mind from the way he glanced at her every now and then but she didn't press him to speak, thinking no conversation was better than conflict and she was enjoying the quiet and the lack of tension and the big night sky which wrapped the truck.

Traveling together like this was both familiar and intimate. Trey on one side, she on the other with TJ in the center.

Trey cleared his throat. "Were you able to reach Lawrence?"

She shook her head. "Tried twice, got his voice mail each time. I left a message the second time."

He was silent for another minute, before shooting her a side glance. "What did you say in the message?"

"That you and TJ needed to catch up and I thought it was a good idea for you to spend Christmas together." She could tell he wanted to ask another question and so she headed him off, adding, "I also left a message for my friend Paige, letting her know everything was okay and that we were with you. I asked her to let my brothers and Aunt Karen know."

"Your family won't be happy."

"I don't know who will be more upset, my brothers or Aunt Karen."

"Your aunt's never liked me."

"She didn't dislike you until she found us naked together in my bedroom."

"I wasn't naked, and you had...a few things...on. Your blouse...your bra..." His voice trailed off and his lips curved in a rueful smile. "You know she wouldn't have come running if you hadn't been loud."

"Don't blame me! How was I to know how good it

would feel? It's your fault for being so…talented…that way."

"We didn't see each other for a while after that."

"Two months I think, which was ridiculous because we'd been dating two years at that point. Did they honestly think you and I weren't going to try anything? That we weren't going to eventually mess around?"

The corner of his mouth quirked and they slipped back into silence, traveling another five miles with memories hanging over them.

She and Trey had grown up together. Hard to remember a time when they weren't together…

"I didn't think you wanted a big wedding," he said, a few minutes later, his attention on the road. "You'd always said that when we got married you just wanted immediate family, something small and intimate."

McKenna didn't immediately reply. She would have preferred a small wedding but Lawrence had wanted to invite all his clients and friends so the wedding grew from fifty to one hundred and then one hundred and fifty, and that was where she put her foot down. One hundred and fifty was plenty for a candle light wedding the last Saturday before Christmas.

"I think the wedding was for Lawrence and the community," she said after a moment. "There are many in Marietta who want closure for me…they want that happy ending."

"And a fancy wedding would give them closure?"

"I think people want me to be happy, and they hoped that by marrying Lawrence, TJ and I would have stability."

"Or maybe they were just glad that Lawrence would keep you away from me."

She started to protest but closed her mouth, swallowing the protest. He was right. He was not Marietta's favorite son.

"I never cared what people thought," she said softly, glancing at him, and taking in his profile with the jutting jaw and firm press of lips. He was leaner than she remembered, and yet bigger, harder. He was carrying a lot of muscle still, but he seemed to have virtually no body fat.

In the light of the truck dash, he glowed, rugged and Hollywood handsome. Black hair, long black lashes, piercing blue eyes, chiseled bone structure.

He'd always been good looking, but in his mid thirties he had a maturity that suited him.

The last vestiges of boy were gone. He was all man. A gorgeous, darkly beautiful man.

When he'd been sentenced to prison she'd thought her heart was permanently broken and so it'd been a surprise when she finally accepted Lawrence's invitation to dinner.

Maybe she was comfortable with Lawrence because he was nothing like Trey.

Lawrence wasn't sexy or sexual. He wasn't hard taut muscle. He wasn't a rancher or a cowboy. He couldn't rope a fence post, much less a steer. And no, he couldn't fix the engine of a car or deliver a calf. He couldn't drive in snow. He couldn't shoot, hunt, fish or build a proper fire.

But he was sweet, and thoughtful, gentle and kind. If he

said he'd be there at seven, he always showed up...five minutes early. If she needed anything, he was there. He treated her like she was the best thing since sliced bread and it felt good to be important and valued.

It felt good to know he'd be there the next day, and the day after, and the day after that.

It felt good not to worry that he'd be out too late, drinking too much, getting heated, instigating fights.

It felt good to be with someone that folks didn't criticize.

"People really thought Lawrence would be a better husband and father than me?" Trey sounded incredulous. "A man who has so little backbone that he allows a five year old to walk all over him?"

"Well, TJ's not just any five year old. He is *your* five year old."

"My point exactly."

She chewed on her lip, thinking, remembering the fight, the trial, the sentence and then those two years she drove twice a month to see him, carting the baby, who was quickly growing into a spirited toddler.

TJ always cried during the drives to the prison, but he cried the most when they left Trey behind. He cried because he didn't know why he had to leave his daddy behind, again, and TJ's tears and grief had worn her down. TJ had been too young to feel so much anguish. He hadn't understood. She couldn't seem to make him understand. And what about when Trey was released?

Would he be there for them then? Did she believe deep down he'd ever be there for them?

She hadn't known anymore.

She hadn't trusted Trey anymore.

She'd come to see him as others saw him—a dominant male, fierce and physical—but a man who was in need of reason and self-control.

She'd finally heard what everyone said....that he was reactive, responding instinctively without regard to risks and consequence, and she'd seen that they were right. He refused to grow up, refused to control his temper, refuse to bend or yield which meant he could never be depended on.

She loved how beautiful he was, remembered how amazing it felt when they were together. Making love with Trey wasn't just sexual, it was emotional and spiritual....or at least it used to be before she was so angry with him. So frustrated and hurt.

And so she'd found the opposite of Trey in Lawrence Joplin, and when Lawrence proposed the third time, she put aside her reservations, telling herself that passion was less important than predictability, and accepted his marriage offer, determined that the future would be different from the past.

But now everything had changed again and instead of being teary and conflicted, she was...calm.

Relieved.

There was that word again. She almost felt a little guilty for feeling relieved that she wasn't marrying Lawrence. And now she wondered if that was why she had felt so many butterflies earlier, at the church. Had she been getting cold feet and she just wouldn't admit it? Had she not wanted to marry him but was too afraid of hurting his feelings to say something?

She hoped she wasn't that much of a coward. She'd been through too much in life to be a doormat...

But no, she wasn't a doormat. She'd stood up to Trey plenty of times, refusing to marry him until he got his act together and grew up and acted like a man.

She'd stood up to her family when they'd pressured her to stop seeing Trey.

She'd ignored the gossip in Marietta when she'd chosen to be a single mom rather than marry a man she didn't think was ready to settle down.

No, she wasn't a doormat. And she had a spine. But she also was tender hearted when it came to those she loved. And she loved Lawrence, but probably more as a friend than a lover and life partner.

Which was why it baffled her that Lawrence had taken it upon himself to tell TJ why his father was in prison. Lawrence had promised her he wouldn't say anything, agreeing to leave it to her so she could tell TJ when she thought the moment was right.

But Lawrence had broken that promise. Why?

And if he'd broken that promise to her, how much others had he not kept?

Chapter Ten

THEY ARRIVED AT Bigfork at a little after midnight, the high full moon reflecting white off Flathead Lake as they drove south fifteen miles on Highway 35 to the little town of Cherry Lake.

If they kept going another eighteen miles they'd come to Polson.

Trey's mom, Catherine Cray, had spent her early years outside Cherry Lake, a member of the Bitterroot Salish tribe that formed part of the Confederated Salish and Kootenai Tribes of the Flathead Nation.

All but the northern tip of Flathead Lake was part of the extensive Flathead Indian Reservation, and when Trey's mother's grandparents died, they left an old cabin on the lower slope of the Mission Mountains, and a couple acres of land to their daughter, hoping she'd return and raise her sons on the land of her ancestors.

Trey's father hadn't minded taking the boys to the cabin with its spectacular view of Flathead Lake for fishing trips, but he wasn't interested in his wife's native ancestry. She wasn't even half Salish and he wasn't about to raise his sons as native this, or that.

Trey hadn't been to the cabin in years, but until recently Cormac visited regularly, and apparently just this past summer Brock had brought Harley and the kids for a ten-day vacation, using the time to rebuild the old stone fireplace, install a new stove in the kitchen, and make a number of smaller repairs.

"Know where we're going now?" Trey asked McKenna as they drove past the turn-off to sleepy little Cherry Lake, a Flathead Lake town that came alive in summer with tourists and the colorful fresh fruit stands dotting the road selling crates of Lamberts, Rainier and Hardy Giant cherries.

"I had a suspicion when you took 83 north," McKenna answered, shifting TJ to free her arm, which had gone numb sometime in the last half hour. "When's the last time you were here?"

"It's been a long time, but you were here with me. It was a couple years before TJ was born."

"I remember," she said softly. They'd driven from Marietta for a long weekend at the cabin in late September. Most of the tourists were gone and the local kids were all in school. It jad felt like they had the lake and town to themselves. "We had fun."

He shot her a swift glance, expression somber. "We did," he agreed. "And we will again."

The last words were spoken so quietly she wasn't sure he'd even said them. She glanced at him but his attention was on the steep private road that wound back to the cabin.

THE KEYS TO the Cray cabin were right where they'd always been, tucked high up the hollowed leg of the wooden grizzly cub gracing the cabin's front porch. Trey unlocked the cabin's front door, flipped on the light switch and was gratified to see light flood the open main room, a combination of living room, dining room and small kitchen.

The one and a half story log cabin had been built in the late 1940's and had just the bare minimum in maintenance until Cormac started paying regular visits ten years ago. The cabin was still rustic, with stacked log walls and exposed trusses in the vaulted ceiling but everything looked clean and weather proofed.

Trey did a quick walk through, flipping on lights in the two downstairs bedrooms and turning on the heater. The windows in both bedrooms were original, and weren't double paned. Once the wooden shutters were removed, the bedrooms would be a lot colder. He hoped the big cedar chest in the master bedroom still held all the sheets, quilts and comforters. They were going to need to make up the beds and get extra blankets on them, too.

He returned to the truck where McKenna and TJ were waiting. "Got the heater on and the lights on," he said. "But we'll need to get the beds made up."

"If you've got clean sheets, I can do that," she said, shivering as she handed TJ over.

"The cedar chest should be full of them."

McKenna lifted her full skirts high as she followed Trey up the path to the cabin. Her heels weren't designed for hiking up a rutted dirt path. "I don't suppose there are any clothes here? I'm not going to want to put this dress back on tomorrow."

"I'm sure we can find something for the night, and then tomorrow we'll go shopping in Cherry Lake, and if Cherry Lake doesn't have it, Polson or Bigfork will."

MCKENNA QUICKLY MADE up both twin beds with sheets and blankets in the smaller bedroom, before taking a sleepy and disoriented TJ to the bathroom where she stripped off his pants, shoes and socks and then tucked him into one of the twin beds in his shirt.

Trey made up the queen size bed in the master bedroom while she put TJ to bed. She'd slept in the master bedroom the last time she was here. It seemed as if they'd spent most of their time at the cabin in bed.

But she wouldn't think about that. There was no point dwelling on the past. She hadn't agreed to let TJ spend Christmas with his dad so she and Trey could rekindle a romance. She wasn't interested in romance. She'd like to be friends with Trey, though. And she'd like to see TJ and Trey have the kind of father-son relationship they both craved.

McKENNA COULD HEAR Trey moving around in the central room, bringing in firewood and stacking it next to the big stone fireplace.

She lay on her side in the narrow twin bed listening to him open and close doors and arrange the firewood.

It was strange lying here, listening to him work. It was one in the morning. Wasn't he tired?

Or was he out there working because he felt all wound up, too?

McKenna turned onto her back and stared at the ceiling. She wasn't sure how she felt, being back at the Cray cabin. This was a place shared by the five Sheenan brothers. They never invited outsiders. It was just for family. When Trey had brought her here that September, they were still newly engaged.

Now she was back and her emotions were all over the place.

It might not have been a good idea, coming here for Christmas.

But then, this Christmas wasn't about her, and what she wanted. This Christmas was about Trey and TJ. This Christmas was about them having a special holiday together.

Restless, she flipped her covers and quilt back, floorboards creaking beneath her bare feet as she went to his bed. Even though Trey had left the wooden blinds closed, slivers of moonlight slipped through the cracks and streaked the log frame.

TJ looked small in the twin bed, his cheek nestled deep into the down pillow, his hair dark on the crisp white pillowcase.

She leaned over and lightly kissed his warm cheek, before tugging the covers higher on his shoulder.

She loved him so much. From the beginning she'd tried to do everything right. She wanted him to have everything a little boy needed. Halloween costumes and Christmas traditions. Swim lessons, summer vacations, Saturday matinee movies.

But despite her best efforts, she hadn't been able to give TJ everything. He didn't have a daddy that was there, and it was the only thing he asked for.

Again and again and again.

A daddy to take him fishing. A daddy for cub scouting. A daddy for wrestling and hugging and loving.

A lump formed in her throat. She'd agreed to marry Lawrence for TJ's sake. It was a terrible thing to admit. She didn't need the company as much as TJ needed a father figure.

She'd thought Lawrence was the answer. At least, she'd hoped he was the answer. But Lawrence and TJ had never really clicked. She could admit that now. She could see that she'd tried to force them to like each other, planning activities to help them get along. She'd thought if she tried hard enough eventually they'd grow fond of each other but it hadn't happened. Lawrence, a forty-year old bachelor when he'd begun dating McKenna, couldn't relate to a headstrong little boy who wasn't interested in learning cribbage and chess. TJ wanted Lawrence to box and run and wrestle. He wanted physical activity not quiet games.

Lawrence criticized McKenna's parenting.

McKenna privately pleaded with TJ to do the activities Lawrence enjoyed so they could all be happy together.

The more pressure McKenna put on TJ to cooperate with Lawrence, the more resistant TJ became to all of Lawrence's suggestions. Lawrence thought it was a problem. But TJ wasn't a problem and he wasn't spoiled or a little monster. He was just himself…active, healthy, busy, smart.

McKenna loved his sense of humor. She loved his personality. She didn't want him to be anybody but himself.

The only times she and Lawrence argued was over how she was raising TJ.

Now, asleep, TJ looked impossibly angelic, and nothing like a little monster. She lightly placed one last kiss on his soft cheek. She could feel his warm breath as she straightened.

Her boy. And Trey's boy.

TJ's lashes fluttered. He opened his eyes and looked up at her. "Mommy, what are you doing?" he asked, his voice rough with sleep.

"Checking on you."

"Where are you sleeping?"

"In here, with you. Now go back to sleep."

"Good night, Mommy."

"Good night, sweet boy."

He closed his eyes and yawned. "I love you."

"I love you, too."

IT WAS LATE, after two in the morning, but Trey couldn't sleep in the big bed in the master bedroom.

He'd taken a hot shower after finishing stacking the firewood and laying a fire for the next morning. And he was physically tired but he couldn't clear his mind long enough to let him relax.

McKenna and TJ were here, under his roof.

It was incredible, so incredible he didn't know how to process it. This morning he'd woken up, sick that he'd lost McKenna, and desperate to make sure he didn't lose TJ, too.

It'd been an intense afternoon and everything that could have gone wrong…didn't.

By some miracle, McKenna and his son were here, with him. Not with Lawrence. By some miracle he had been given a chance…

It was time he redeemed himself.

And he would.

God…fate…whatever you called it… had given him this opportunity, and this time Trey wouldn't blow it.

He loved his family. He needed his family. And he was prepared to do whatever it took to prove that he was here for them, too.

EVEN THOUGH TREY had fallen asleep late, he was up early to turn up the heat and light the fire. He was lucky that there were clothes he could wear—jeans and t-shirts and flannel shirts, boots and a pair of running shoes, left by his brothers.

There was nothing for TJ to wear in any of the cabin closets but McKenna could maybe get away with a pair of sweat pants and a flannel shirt and the running shoes.

He left the clothes folded outside their bedroom door before grabbing his keys and driving into town to pick up coffee, eggs, bread, milk, butter, bacon and juice from the twenty-four hour convenience store attached to the gas station. He was just about to walk out when he spotted a couple bright red sweatshirts with the slogan Stay and Play at Cherry Lake folded up on a shelf with other souvenir items. The smallest size they had was a Youth Medium but Trey grabbed it, thinking it would at least give TJ something warm to wear.

Back at the cabin, he stoked the fire, added another log, and then made coffee in the old coffee machine he found in one of the kitchen cupboards.

He was busy frying bacon and whisking eggs when the bedroom door opened and McKenna appeared, still wearing the red flannel shirt from Trey's truck.

And from the looks of it, only wearing the red flannel shirt.

"Sleep okay?" Trey asked, whisking the eggs more vigorously, forcing himself to look away. She was almost too beautiful, her long hair loose and spilling over her shoulders, the soft flannel fabric outlining the swell of her breasts and the shirt hem reaching only to mid thigh, leaving her long shapely legs gloriously bare.

"Better than you, I think," she answered, smiling and crossing behind him to check the coffee. "Can I have a cup?"

"Please do."

"Have you had any yet?"

"No. It has only just finished brewing."

She opened the upper cabinet doors until she found two mugs and rinsed them out at the sink before filling them. The coffee was hot and she set a steaming cup at his elbow. "You don't know how much I wanted this," she said, circling her cup with her hands. "I don't do well without my coffee in the morning."

He smiled ruefully. "I remembered."

She leaned against the counter, watching him flip the sizzling bacon. "I thought I would be freezing this morning but you've made it toasty warm in here."

"Didn't want you and TJ cold."

"You've been up for a while, haven't you?"

"Hard to sleep with so much on my mind."

She sipped her coffee, and a long lock red hair fell forward. Carelessly she pushed it back, anchoring the curl behind an ear. "What's on your mind?"

He placed another skillet on the stove, turned on the burner, and added butter to the pan. "I want you and TJ happy," he said after a moment.

"TJ's happy."

He shot her a look over his shoulder. "I want you happy, too."

She didn't look at him. She stared at the pan, watching the butter melt. "We're here for TJ. This is about him."

"Not for me."

"Trey, it's important I be straight with you. I want to be fair to you. I'm not interested in romance, or a relationship with you. But I would like to be friends. Good friends. That way we can raise TJ amicably, without tension."

"I agree."

"But a romantic or sexual relationship would just complicate everything. You know it would. The sex thing always gets us in trouble."

He'd learned a lot living for the past four years with little personal space and zero privacy. He'd learned to check his emotions by removing himself from a situation. He did that now, aware that this wasn't about him, but her, and what she needed. McKenna needed to feel safe. She needed space. She needed time. No problem.

He nodded as he poured the beaten eggs into the skillet with the melted butter. "You're right," he said. "The sex was a problem."

Her jaw dropped ever so slightly. "You think so?"

"I do." He put the ceramic bowl in the sink and rinsed it out before reaching for one of the green checked dishtowels to dry his hands. "The problem is that the physical side of our relationship was too good. Making love felt so natural that I think we expected the rest of our relationship to be that way." He glanced at her. "Now, I don't regret the sex. It was hot. Pretty damn amazing. You know how much I love your body, but maybe the touching and kissing got in the way."

She blinked. "Wow. I'm….shocked. But in a good way."

"That's good." He smiled at her. "It's nice that we are on the same page."

She pushed her hand through her hair, shoving it back from her face, and he told himself he hadn't noticed the way her shirt cupped her breasts or lifted to reveal several inches of pale creamy skin high on her thigh.

They weren't lovers anymore. They were friends. Platonic friends. Platonic friends who didn't have fringe benefits. He'd make sure of that. And he'd be the best platonic friend she ever had. So good that she'd be the one to begging to get back into his bed.

He gestured to the pile of clothes still stacked outside her door. "I picked up a sweatshirt for TJ at the convenience store, and found some clothes that belong to one of my brothers that will get you covered and warm until we can go shopping after breakfast. Feel free to top off your coffee before you shower and dress. I'm sure you'll feel far more comfortable and less naked once you're out of that old shirt and dressed."

She stared at him a moment, and then nodded. "Sounds like a plan."

Chapter Eleven

I T WAS THE twenty-first of December, the last Sunday before Christmas, and Cherry Lake sparkled beneath the sunlit blue sky, Main Street picture book pretty with festive green boughs and red ribbons on the lights and carols playing from invisible speakers. The cafes and shops lining the street were perfectly festive, too, decorated with fragrant wreaths, frosted windows, and charming holiday displays.

But trying to find everything they needed in Cherry Lake took some creativity and visits to six different stores to purchase the necessary undergarments, outer garments, shoes and coats. In the past, Trey had dragged his feet on shopping trips, but his patience and good spirits this morning amazed McKenna. He carried all the bags, kept TJ entertained, and hummed along with the carols, reminding her that he had a gorgeous voice.

He was gorgeous, too, and she wasn't the only one who'd noticed. Women in the shops stared appreciatively, while others passing them on Main Street, cast swift, furtive second and third glances.

McKenna had forgotten what it felt like to be out with a man that drew tons of female admiration. Lawrence had been pleasant looking, attractive in that wholesome kind of way, but Trey was in a whole other league. Trey was darkly beautiful, sinfully beautiful, and she understood why women looked.

Men weren't that handsome in real life.

Men weren't that tall and muscular. They didn't have hair that thick and dark or eyes that brilliant a blue. Their cheekbones weren't that high or their jaws that chiseled. They didn't flash dimples when they laughed. Their laughter and voices didn't rumble in their chests. They simply weren't made so perfectly.

They weren't.

But Trey was. And his brother Troy. However, Troy wasn't Trey, and McKenna had only ever had eyes for Trey since seeing him at Marietta High, surrounded by a group of guys that looked like they were up to no good.

And they weren't. Trey's friends cut class, showed up drunk or stoned, and spent more time in the front office than in class.

McKenna shouldn't have been intrigued. She shouldn't have been attracted to someone so obviously bad.

But when Trey looked at her, his gaze would always soften, his expression gentling. It happened so quickly she didn't know if he was even conscious that his expression changed, and he didn't look at anyone else that way. She knew because she watched him. She watched him a lot, fascinated by the way he carried himself, and the way others whispered about him, saying he was dangerous, reckless, saying he didn't care about anybody, saying he would probably die young.

She didn't want him to die young. She wanted him to play it safer. She wanted him to look at her more. She loved seeing how his hard, handsome features transformed when he saw her...lips curving, blue eyes creasing.

He might not enjoy school, but he was smart, and tough, and he made her feel safe.

He made her feel pretty, too.

And he might never ask her out, but she was his. They both knew it.

"What?" he asked, shooting her a quick glance, black eyebrows lifting.

"Nothing," she answered, amazed that seventeen years later she still felt so connected to him.

"You're smiling."

"You're humming," she said. "Christmas *carols*."

"I like Christmas carols."

"You're humming the sacred ones."

"I can't like songs with a little substance?"

His innocent expression, and his blue eyes, suddenly so guileless, made her laugh out loud. "I know you. I know who you are."

"And who am I, darlin'?"

She looked up into his eyes, and he let her look, inviting her in, and she could have stood there all day, feeling close to him, feeling connected.

Heart, mind, soul.

And then someone tried to get past and accidentally bumped into McKenna and McKenna tripped a bit over TJ and the spell was broken.

The old gentleman who bumped into her apologized and McKenna said no, it was her fault, and blushing, she felt like a fool.

She wasn't being smart.

She wasn't being careful.

Trey Sheenan might be gorgeous and charismatic but he wasn't good for her. He wasn't settled or stable. She couldn't let him back in, couldn't drop her defenses.

They could be friends. And friendly. But that was all.

No romance, no love, no sex, no happy ever after.

No happy ever after. It didn't exist. Not with him.

AFTER CLOTHES SHOPPING they stopped for lunch at one of the little cafes on Main Street. Trey asked TJ what he wanted for Christmas, and once TJ started in, he didn't stop. He hadn't seen Santa yet, and he hadn't sent him a letter but usually if he left him a note at Christmas Santa brought him what he wanted, although last year he wanted holsters and pistols and Santa didn't bring those. Santa never brought guns. Or any fighting things. TJ was disappointed that Santa wouldn't bring him fighting things when everyone else got them. Didn't Santa know he was a boy, not a girl?

McKenna could feel Trey's eyes on her now and then while TJ talked.

She told herself she didn't want to know what he was thinking. She told herself she was happy to keep distance between them. Distance was good. Distance was smart.

After lunch they stopped at the local grocery store and Trey thrust a wad of bills in her hand and told her to go get whatever she wanted while he and TJ went to the hardware store next door and picked up a few things for the cabin.

McKenna didn't want to be in the grocery store while Trey and TJ shopped at the hardware store. She liked being with them. She liked their energy and the way they talked and teased. It was boisterous and brash and fun. She'd forgotten how much fun Trey had always been. Trey had so much energy and good humor. He liked to laugh. He'd always loved to make her laugh, and now his focus was on TJ and TJ was eating it up.

It would be silly to be jealous of TJ. He was Trey's son. He deserved Trey's undivided attention. But she knew what it felt like to be the focus of Trey's attention. She knew how special she used to feel...

Cart full, she waited in line to check out and then pushed the cart outside, heading for Trey's truck.

Trey and TJ were already in the truck waiting for her,

and Trey stepped out and immediately began loading up the back with the groceries.

"What did you buy?" she asked him, glancing at the dozen paper bags with the hardware logo on the front.

"Tools, nails, screws, light bulbs, wood glue, extension cords. How about you?"

"Steaks, potatoes, vegetables, peanut butter, flour, sugar, salt."

"Chocolate chips?" he asked hopefully. "Gingerbread mix?"

"You got a little sweet tooth, Sheenan?"

"Not usually, Mac. But for some reason when you're around, I do."

He'd said it quietly, casually, but the words wrapped around her heart and stole her breath.

It wasn't fair how much she'd missed this—*him*—these past few years. She'd missed the banter and the teasing and his sexy laugh and the way he used to kiss her so slow, kiss her until she was dizzy and mindless and so perfectly content, wanting nothing more than to share a life with him.

"I think that's it," she said breathlessly, placing the last bag in the back and straightening. "I'll just take the cart back—"

"I've got it. You get in with TJ."

"I can do it—"

"I've got it, Mac. Please get in. Get warm. Be safe."

BE SAFE.

Be safe.

The words played in her head during the ten minute drive from town to Cray Road and up the winding private road to the cabin.

Be safe, she heard as she unpacked the groceries.

Be safe, she heard as TJ and Trey disappeared up into the attic, with TJ giggling and whispering and Trey hushing him saying, *Sssh. You don't want to ruin the surprise.*

She couldn't figure out why those words were bothering her so much. Why should she mind him saying be safe? Why should that be a bad thing?

And then it hit her—he was the one who needed to be safe.

He was the one who took the chances.

He was the one who'd left her and TJ alone for four years because he was the one who wasn't safe.

If she wanted to be safe, then she needed Lawrence, or someone like Lawrence, in her life. She needed someone who sold insurance and didn't take risks. Someone who insisted on slow and safe. Someone who preferred predictable. Someone who avoided extremes and change and adrenalin and danger.

But when all was said and done, she hadn't really wanted Lawrence, or someone like Lawrence.

How was she to ever fall in love with anyone else when Trey still possessed her heart?

WHILE MCKENNA BAKED an easy pumpkin bread and made chewy molasses cookies, Trey and TJ worked outside putting something together. She heard hammering and sawing and the scrape of metal. She wondered if it was an old sled they'd found, but she didn't know what they'd do with a sled since there was no snow on the ground, and she would have gone outside to see what they were working on but she'd been given strict instructions to stay inside and be *surprised*.

And so she was baking, waiting to be surprised, and smiling whenever she heard TJ's high bright peal of laughter. He was so happy today. He was in his element helping Trey drag boxes from the attic, carrying paper bags of stuff from the truck, tramping in and out getting cups of hot cocoa for 'the men', making noise, creating chaos. Having fun.

Finally, the front door banged open again and TJ shouted for her to close her eyes and not peek.

"I'm making cookies," she shouted back. "I have to peek."

"Just keep your eyes closed two minutes," Trey answered.

And so she squeezed her eyes shut and propped her chin in her hands and waited. She knew what it was by the smell, even without the sound of branches brushing and scraping the front door.

A tree. They were bringing in a Christmas tree.

"Are you looking?" TJ asked.

"No." But her lips curved and she was smiling, happy for TJ. This was a special Christmas. This was exactly the kind of Christmas he needed.

Muffled voices and whispers and an ouch came from the main room.

"Okay," TJ said after a moment of some huffing and puffing. "Open your eyes!"

She opened her eyes and a tall douglas fir filled one corner of the living room. This was not a fat, full perfectly shaped tree from a Christmas tree farm, but an eight foot tree that had been cut from the Cray land, that had character along with gaps between some of the branches.

"What do you think, Mom?" TJ asked, beaming. "Pretty nice, huh?"

She nodded and smiled back. "One of the nicest trees I've ever seen."

The boxes TJ and Trey had brought down from the attic contained old strings of lights and dozens of vintage glass ornaments.

While the pumpkin bread cooled and the molasses cookies baked, McKenna helped Trey and TJ put lights on the tree—not the old ones from the attic, but the box of new lights Trey had bought today from the hardware store—and then used the new ornament hooks to hang the beautiful vintage ornaments on the tree, the tarnished glass balls a mix of silver, white, and gold, as well as some that were a soft rose and aqua blue. They glittered, sparkled and shone on the green branches of the fresh douglas fir.

After they were done, Trey turned off the living room

lamps to admire their handiwork. Outside it was dusk and the lavender shadows pressed against the windows. Inside the fire burned and glowed and the tree gleamed with balls of color and the strings of white miniature lights.

"All we need are some stockings and Santa can come," Trey said.

"Santa will find us here?" TJ asked.

"Of course." Trey paused. "If you were a good boy. Were you a good boy this year?"

TJ was silent a long moment. "Most the time," he said finally, his voice uncertain. "Does that count?"

Trey laughed. "Absolutely." He glanced at McKenna, still grinning. "Don't you think, Mac?"

"Yes. When it comes to you two. It's got to. Otherwise, we'd never have Christmas or visits from Santa Claus."

LATE THAT NIGHT, after dinner and dishes, they sat in the living room admiring the tree, enjoying the fire. Trey told TJ stories about when he was a boy and how he and his brothers would go look for the perfect tree and how they'd always end up fighting and one or more would return home with a bloody nose, or worse.

TJ loved the stories, and he asked questions about who was stronger—Uncle Brock or Uncle Cormac, and who ran faster, Uncle Troy or Uncle Dillon, and McKenna sat curled up in one of the threadbare armchairs listening to Trey answer all of TJ's questions. He was so patient with his son, so incredibly sweet, and it moved her more than words could say.

Lawrence had tolerated TJ but he'd never loved him. He'd never enjoyed him. He'd never cared about the things that interested TJ...not the way Trey did.

And she got the feeling watching Trey with TJ that if he'd met her, and she'd been a single mom to TJ, Trey would have cared about her son. He would have tried to not merely parent him and keep him safe, but would have laughed and played. Trey would always engage and entertain. Trey would make a child's life...fun.

And fun mattered.

Happiness mattered.

Safety and stability was important, but what was a stable, safe life without humor and excitement and pleasure?

One of the reasons she'd loved Trey was that he'd always made her laugh. He'd made her giggle and smile and feel good.

Those things mattered.

Watching Trey and TJ together now she felt as if she could see Trey, truly see him, all the way through to his soul.

And no, his soul wasn't shiny and silver bright, but tarnished like the vintage balls on the tree, and perhaps even bruised and broken, marked with jagged cuts and welts and scars.

Yet for all those scars and dull marks, there was something so very beautiful in him. He was alive, and strong, and deep.

But then, wasn't that the appeal from the beginning. That he was flawed and real? That he was open and honest? *Human.*

He'd never tried to cover up his weaknesses. He'd never sugar-coated anything for anyone, and he certainly had never pretended to be a perfect man, one of those romance novel heroes....all good and pure, the idealized boyfriend every girl wanted.

No. He wasn't that great, stand up guy.

But it hadn't mattered. She'd loved him anyway, as even broken and flawed, he'd felt like hers.

She'd been the one to seduce him. She'd been the one to push his buttons, wanting him to treat her like a woman, not a girl. Wanting him to be hot and demanding, sensual and physical.

He'd wanted to marry her ever since he graduated from high school. He'd wanted to do the right thing by her, but she refused to marry him until he stopped fighting and drinking and driving and staying out late causing trouble with 'the boys'. She didn't like that he was one person with her, and then this street-tough alpha with everyone else. Why couldn't he be as kind and charming with everyone as he was with her? Why couldn't he try harder to fit in? Settle down? Be good?

They'd fought about his behavior for years...

Don't cause trouble. Don't stay out too late. Don't drink too much because you'll just end up doing something stupid...

But he liked who he was and he wasn't interested in changing. He enjoyed all the things she was afraid of...the fist fights, the late nights, the rowdy groups of guys he hung out with. He enjoyed being tough, strong, slightly danger-ous.

"This is who I am," he'd told her more than once. "This is what I am."

"Someday something will happen," she'd answer. "Someday something beyond your control."

And then it had happened. The fight at the Wolf Den, with its disastrous results. Bradley Warner had died after falling and striking his head on the edge of the bar, and Trey was arrested and charged with manslaughter.

It didn't matter that Trey had intervened to protect Bradley's pregnant girlfriend from Bradley's fists. It didn't matter that witnesses said that Trey had only thrown a few punches and had never lost control. It didn't matter that Trey was supposed to be the good guy and Brad was the bad guy. Because Brad died and Trey was responsible and Trey had to pay.

There were consequences for fighting.

Consequences for not following rules.

Consequences for being tough and physical and fearless.

For the past two years McKenna had told herself that she was rejecting Trey because she didn't want TJ to grow up like him, but suddenly she knew she'd wronged them, both of them.

There was so much good in Trey, and so much good in TJ.

She couldn't reject one without rejecting the other and suddenly she wasn't so sure that being good, being safe, was the right answer.

She didn't want to be stupid and didn't want danger, but she wanted more than safe, wanted more than predictable.

She wanted teasing and smiles, love and laughter.

She wanted her heart back.

She wanted her life back.

She wanted Trey and TJ together.

With her.

Together a family with her.

But she was scared. She was scared that if she let down her guard, if she allowed Trey back in, something bad could happen—again—and she could lose him, and her heart, and her happiness all over. Again.

Chapter Twelve

McKENNA WOKE UP to the incessant trilling and drumming of a bird outside her cabin window. It had been going on and on and she'd tried to ignore it and fall back asleep but it wasn't happening, not while the bird kept thrumming and kuk-kuk-kuking outside the window.

Climbing from bed she went to the small window and pushed back the shutter. She shivered in her pajamas, which was really just a man's t-shirt, X-Large, and craned her head to try to find the offending bird. The sun was just starting to rise and she couldn't see a bird, but she could still hear it, *kuk-kuk-kuking,* over and over.

McKenna bumped into Trey in the hallway. He was fully dressed and she tugged the hem of the t-shirt down, trying to cover herself.

"You're up early," he said.

"What time is it?" she asked, thinking that the t-shirt had seemed perfectly roomy and modest last night but seemed to cover far less of her now.

"Not quite six."

"I didn't want to be awake this early," she answered, smothering a yawn. "But there is the most annoying bird outside—"

"Our resident woodpecker. I heard it, too."

"It's been making noise half the night."

"The pileated woodpeckers do. Our woods are full of them. They love the old growth trees."

"Great."

He must have noticed that she kept tugging on the hem of her t-shirt. "Aren't you wearing panties?"

"Yes. Why?"

"You're acting excessively virginal, Mac," he said, sounding amused.

"Be quiet. Go shave. Or better yet, be useful and make some coffee."

"I have, and it's waiting for you, Princess. Or was I supposed to bring it to you in bed?"

"*No.*" And yet the moment he said the word bed, her imagination sparked, creating all sorts of wanton images in her head. Images she didn't want or need. Because when it came to making love with Trey, reality was so much better than fantasy. He was that good. And he felt that good, and no, she'd never slept with any other man than Trey, so she didn't know if it'd be that good with someone else, but honestly, she hadn't wanted to find out.

Trey had been her only one.

Although once she married Lawrence, she would have obviously had to make love to him. She suppressed a faint shudder. She hadn't been looking forward to that.

Although she was pretty sure he had.

She crossed her arms over her chest, hiding her breasts. "Did any of your brothers ever leave a robe behind?"

"Nope, but I did find an old wool cardigan. It's huge, XXL, and rather moth eaten but it could be a robe on you."

"I'll take it. Thank you."

She was in the kitchen filling her cup when he returned with a grey, beige and cream knit sweater with an Indian motif.

"That's beautiful," she said, taking the wool sweater from him and examining the intricate Indian design.

"My great Grandmother Cray made it. My mother said she made hundreds of sweaters and blankets during her life to help pay bills. Cormac has been able to track down a few in antique stores and on eBay as her stitches and designs are different from the Coastal Salish, but this sweater has been in the family forever. It was probably made for one of my uncles, or even my great grandfather."

"It should be in a museum."

"No, it shouldn't. It was made for family, it should be worn by family."

"But I'm not—"

"Yes, you are. You're my family. You'll always be family to me."

She undid the sturdy buttons and slipped one arm in and then the other. The sweater was heavy and long, and a little bit itchy, but it was a Cray family heirloom, and she could feel the history in it, and the love.

Her eyes suddenly burned and she looked down, focusing on working the wood buttons through the holes. "Do you ever think about that side of your family?" she asked, voice husky. "Do you ever think that maybe the reason you felt like such an outsider in Marietta was because you take after the Crays? That maybe you were never meant to be cooped up in classrooms and offices but outside...free?"

He didn't immediately answer and she looked up, to find him staring hard at her, a strange expression on his face.

"What?" she whispered. "Was that a bad thing to say?"

"My mom used to say that," he said quietly. "She said that Troy and I might be identical twins, but he'd inherited the Sheenan blood and I'd inherited the Crays." His mouth curved but the smile didn't reach his eyes. "Every time I got in trouble when I was little, every time my dad took the belt to me, or a switch, she would apologize to me, saying that we needed to forgive my father for not understanding who I was, and being unable to recognize my spirit."

His powerful shoulders shifted uncomfortably. "I didn't know what to think when I was younger. Dad didn't recognize Mom's Native American heritage. He didn't want a wife that was 'mixed', and forbad her from telling us stories about Indian folklore and customs. But now and then when I couldn't sleep, I'd go find her, and inevitably those were the nights my father was out and my mother would be awake, staring out the window, looking westward."

Trey glanced down at McKenna, expression pensive. "I didn't understand then how deeply lonely my mother was. She never talked about her loneliness but looking back, we all see it—her sons—and it's hard to realize how much she gave to us and how little she got back—"

"I don't think that's a fair assessment," McKenna interrupted. "Children are not responsible for meeting their parents' needs."

"Maybe not when they are young, but by high school, I should have been more aware, more sensitive. Instead I was at my most rebellious."

"Because you were a teenager, filled with testosterone!"

He shrugged. "I wish you could have heard her stories. I wish I had recorded them or written them down because on those nights when my father was gone, she would talk about the Salish, the Kootenai and the Pend d'Oreille Tribes and how their beliefs about life were so different from the righteous Christians that only talked to God in Church. She said for the Flathead tribes, spirit was everywhere, and that all things were connected and to be respected, plants, rocks, animals, people. She said it was hard to find peace when one simply used things selfishly, and never gave back to the earth. She said the land wasn't there simply to be stripped, but to be protected. The trees and animals have a right to exist.

Man is to recognize the spirit in each of them."

McKenna swallowed around the lump forming in her throat. "But you didn't need to record her stories to remember them. You've remembered."

"I miss her."

She went to him then, and wrapped her arms around his waist and held him, hugging him, knowing he needed to feel her—his mother's love—and if he couldn't have that, he could have her love.

Because she would always love him.

And she had always seen his spirit—and it was good. Yes, he had a wild streak, and he might not ever be completely tamed, but maybe that was who he was meant to be? Beautiful, fierce, and protective.

"She's still with you," McKenna whispered. "Especially here. I can feel her here."

Trey wrapped his arms around her and held her for a moment, before placing a kiss on the top of her head and breaking free.

"There is supposed to be a storm coming in tonight," he said gruffly. "I'm going to go have a look at the generator, make sure it's in working order." And then he was gone, disappearing quickly out the front door.

IT'D BEEN A dry and cold December in much of Montana, with freezing conditions but very little snow. It had snowed hard early in the month but whatever remained in the valleys was now compacted and brown.

With Christmas Eve just three days away, everyone was ready for fresh snow, saying it wouldn't be Christmas without a dusting of powdery white, but the storm coming was supposed to be a big one, with a foot or two of snow falling steadily throughout the night, making it difficult for the snowplows to keep up.

A foot of snow was a lot for Cherry Lake, and the record for heaviest snowfall in one day was sixteen inches back in December of 1929. No one wanted a foot of snow, not so close to Christmas when there was still so much shopping to do and last minute presents to mail.

Trey chopped more firewood and had the generator ready, then stood in the kitchen with McKenna making a list of emergency supplies, although neither of them were too worried, having grown up on isolated Paradise Valley ranches where winter storms routinely knocked out power, forcing families to adapt and make do.

McKenna wanted more milk and eggs, bread, lunchmeat and cheese along with tea, hot cocoa and ingredients for simple dinners for the next couple of nights.

Trey added candles, flashlights, and batteries. He glanced at the list and then to the living room where Trey was stretched out by the fire, staring at the tree. "What about stockings and presents for TJ?" he asked, dropping his voice. "We don't have anything for him, do we?"

"I have gifts for him in Marietta, not here," she said.

"But we're here...unless you're thinking you want to head back early?"

She glanced outside, at the sky, which was patchy with clouds. It didn't look bad now. "Try to beat it, you mean?"

"We wouldn't beat it. We'd be driving through it."

She wrinkled her nose. "But why do that? There's no reason to take extra risks when we could have a cozy Christmas here. We just need to do some shopping, pick up a few things so he has a stocking for Christmas morning and some gifts to open."

Trey nodded and McKenna checked her smile as Trey added, *Buy Toys and Wrapping Paper*, to the bottom of their list.

"I could even do some shopping if you wanted to take him to a matinee movie," she said. "I know there's a theatre showing kids movies in Bigfork. I could drop you two off at the movies and then shop and get all the errands done and then come back for you."

"Or we could divide the errands up and I go do some shopping for TJ now, and then come back and get you two, and then we all head to Bigfork." He looked at her, expression earnest. "It's not that I don't trust you to buy good things, but I really want to pick out something for him, some toys for him from me. Haven't been able to do that since he was born."

His words made her chest tighten and ache.

She loved how much he loved their son. "That's a great

idea," she said. "You shop, I'll make him lunch, and that way when you return, we'll be ready to go."

TREY KNEW HE didn't have a lot of time to shop and it'd been years since he'd been able to buy gifts for TJ and McKenna. As he drove to Cherry Lake he tried to remember all the shops downtown, thinking there had to be a toy store somewhere. He couldn't recall seeing one, but that hadn't been their focus when they'd gone shopping yesterday.

And McKenna...what could he give her? What did she need?

She wasn't one of those women who loved fancy things. She didn't collect jewelry or like high fashion. She did enjoy art but a painting didn't seem like the right kind of gift after not giving her anything for a number of years.

It seemed as if everyone had come to town to finish shopping today. Town was crowded, and parking on Main Street non-existent. Trey parked a few blocks down, by the small post office, and walked back to the shops, sticking his head in any that looked kid-friendly.

Trey found red and green and cream knit stockings at one of the artsy stores. They had three left and he wanted to buy all three and hang them all from the stone fireplace but it seemed silly to buy himself a stocking. He was a man, he didn't need a stocking. But he wanted one for TJ and he'd love to fill one for McKenna even if it was just with tea and some jars of the local cherry flavored honey.

He ended up buying two and headed next door to the colorful candy shoppe that sold fresh saltwater taffy and homemade fudge. He bought taffy and a big lollipop for TJ's stocking and rich creamy blocks of marshmallow-studded fudge for Christmas Eve, hoping TJ liked marshmallows and fudge, unable to imagine a five year old that didn't. But it was an uncomfortable thing realizing he didn't know what his son liked. There were so many things Trey needed to discover and he looked forward to the day where he knew his son as well as McKenna...if not better.

The lady in the candy shoppe told Trey where to find a toy store and Trey headed there next. Again he wasn't sure what kinds of games and toys TJ liked, and felt hopelessly out of depth as he stared at the shelves filled with dolls and fairies, forest animals and farms, Lincoln Logs, puzzles, Duplo, Lego, robots, acrylic tubes and cylinders and other kinds of building blocks.

The sales clerk approached him. "Can I help you find something?"

Trey nodded, perplexed by all the choices. "I'm looking for something for my son," he said. "He's five."

"And what does he like to do?"

Trey rubbed the back of his neck. "I'm not sure."

"Does he have any favorite hobbies?"

"I uh...don't know."

The lady looked perplexed. "Is he into arts and crafts...?"

"I don't think so."

"Does he like costumes and to dress up?"

Trey frowned. "I don't think so. But I don't really know." He chafed at her baffled gaze. "I've been…gone," he said shortly. "I haven't seen him for years."

Her expression cleared. "You just got back from overseas. Bless you, dear, and thank you for your service to the country."

Trey felt sick. He wanted to correct her but couldn't bring himself to extend the conversation a moment longer than necessary. "Can you just show me the toys that are appropriate for five year old boys?"

"Of course. Right here." She led him down a few feet and tapped the shelf "These are all excellent choices. Legos, Ninja turtles, Power Rangers—they remain popular year after year—Transformers, Transformer dinosaurs or bots as some people call them." She pointed to another shelf. "Robots, Hot Wheels, army men—" she broke off to give him a warm smile. "—and then all the Nerf guns and mega blasters. Some parents are funny about giving toy guns but in my experience, most Montana boys love them. We are a hunting and fishing state!"

Trey thanked her for her help, ready to do make some decisions on his own but the sales woman seemed inclined to stay, and chat. "Now, I was one of those parents who didn't want to give toy guns," she said. "But my sons found a way to make guns anyway with their Tinker Toys and Lincoln Logs. Finally one day I thought enough, a boy is a boy, let him be a boy—"

"Thank you," Trey interrupted kindly, but firmly. "You have been so helpful. I'll bring my purchases up to the counter. Will you be the one at the register?"

"I will."

"Perfect. Then I can show you what I've picked out."

Trey was on his way to the truck, his arms filled with plastic bags and wrapped packages when he passed an artsy looking little shop named Montana Hearts that featured glazed mugs and pottery, sculpture and paintings and what looked like handmade jewelry.

It was the jewelry display in the window that caught his attention and made him stop, and then go inside.

"The necklace with the brass angel," he said. "Can I see that?"

"It looks like brass, doesn't it?" the young woman said, leaving the counter to head for the display. "But it's actually standard yellow gold with a pink gold overlay, kind of like Black Hills gold, but we can't call it that since it's not made in South Dakota." She reached into the display and lifted the necklace with the angel out. "I love this. It's so delicate and unusual. It reminds me of a Christmas ornament."

She placed the angel in his open palm and he studied the little angel's swirl of skirt and sweep of halo and wings. She looked so much like the brass angel ornaments he'd bought from McKenna her freshman year of high school. "She's pretty," he said.

"Handmade by a local artisan. We also have another one that's with the same angel, but she's more gold than pink and instead or a harp, she's holding a dark blue Montana sapphire. It's really gorgeous. It's probably my favorite thing we have in the shop."

"That's the one I want."

"It's rather pricey. It's real gold and a genuine sapphire—"

"That's fine. It's perfect. It's exactly what I've been looking for."

Chapter Thirteen

R ETURNING TO THE cabin Trey tucked the bags and
presents in the closet in the master bedroom and then
helped TJ into his coat before doing up the zipper.

TJ ran outside to climb in the truck and Trey and
McKenna followed more slowly.

"Looks like you had some success," she said.

Trey nodded. "It was hard at first. I wasn't sure what TJ
would want but I ended up buying some Legos and then I
spotted these sets of miniature tin soldiers at the antique
store next door to the post office. There are actually two
armies, one in red and one in blue. It's something I would
have liked when I was a kid. It has cannons and guys with
flags and guys on horses, too."

"I think he'll love it."

"Do you?" Trey looked uncertain. "I wasn't sure. So I
also got him this Transformer dinosaur thing just in case."

"TJ is just so happy to have you here. The presents don't
matter."

"It's Christmas, of course they matter."

"What about stocking stuffers? Find anything?"

"I found a stocking and picked up some little things—candy, silly putty and matchbox cars—but you might want to get a few things, too."

"Will do."

He hesitated on the bottom step. "Oh, and Mine Craft. I looked for them everywhere. Couldn't find anything and I'd really hoped to get him one of those Enderman guys."

"You're spoiling him. It's not necessary."

"I'm excited about Christmas."

She smiled. "I know. And so am I. It's going to be fun to watch him open his gifts together."

Trey gave his keys a jingle. "We still need wrapping paper, though. I forgot all about that."

"No worries. Anything else?"

"If you can find a Mine Craft Enderman… can you pick it up for me?"

Her smile grew. "Yes, I will, and don't worry, Henchman, it'll be from you."

IT BEGAN TO snow mid afternoon while McKenna was in the grocery store. She was heading for the check out when she saw the first fat flakes flutter down.

The clerk noticed the snow, too. "Supposed to be the biggest storm of the year. At least one foot tonight, maybe more."

"I heard it's unusual to get that much snow here at one time," McKenna said, taking another quick look over her shopping check list to make sure she hadn't forgotten anything.

"You're not from here?"

"From Marietta." She saw the clerk's puzzled expression. "Between Bozeman and West Yellowstone."

"You get some cold weather."

"We do," McKenna agreed.

"We get off easier, here, protected by the Mission Mountains, and then the lake itself keeps things warmer."

"Does it?" McKenna asked, helping bag up the groceries.

"It's our secret," the clerk answered with a wink. "We're far more temperate than the rest of the state. Great summers, mild winters, but don't tell anyone. We like our quiet little community."

The snow was falling thicker and faster as McKenna drove from the grocery store through downtown Bigfork, windshield wipes scraping back and forth to clear her vision. She scanned the storefronts, looking for a shop that might carry the Mine Craft toys for TJ. There was a toy shop a couple blocks from the movie theater. McKenna snagged a parking spot out front and headed into the store.

"Sold out of all the Mine Craft figurines we had, and didn't get any of the stuffed toys in this year," the teenage boy answered, "but we do have a youth backpack with a Creeper and a Zombie on it. How old is the kid?"

"Five," McKenna said.

"Would he like a backpack?" The teenager scratched the side of his nose. "Does anyone like backpacks? Hard to say. How much does he like Mine Craft?"

"A lot."

"Then he'll like it. I mean, the Zombie and Creeper are both green and the backpack is black. So that's kind of cool, you know?"

McKenna agreed and was at the counter paying for the backpack, keeping one eye on the snow outside which was coming down even faster now, when she spotted a green and white knit stocking hanging from the counter overflowing with packages of Moose poop (chocolate nuggets) and candy coal (licorice). Over the stocking hung a small sign, *For Those on Santa's Naughty List.*

McKenna smiled to herself. "Is this for sale?" she asked.

"Yep. Want it?"

"Yes." She plucked the stocking off the hook and handed it to him. "It's perfect."

THE THICK LACY flakes fell in heavy swirls as McKenna pulled up in front of the movie theater to pick Trey and TJ up. She slid all the way over on the bench seat so Trey could lift TJ into the truck for his middle spot.

"How are the roads?" Trey asked, climbing in and closing the door.

"Good. The snow is sticking but it's powdery so there is

no problem." She buckled TJ's seat belt. "How was the movie?"

"Awesome," TJ said, "And we had popcorn and candy."

"Let me guess," she said. "Red Vines?"

"How did you know?"

"That's always been your daddy's favorite at the movies, and what we had when he and I went on dates back in high school."

"They had Red Vines all the way back then?"

She smiled and tweaked his nose. "It wasn't that long ago."

"Was I born then?"

"No."

"Then that was a long time ago."

IT CONTINUED TO snow steadily the rest of the afternoon, with the snow piling up outside on the wooden railing of the deck, burying the shrubs outside the cabin door. When they first arrived back at the cabin, Trey had made several trips outside to bring in enough firewood to see them through the night, and now they sat at the pine dining table playing Go Fish with an old deck of cards Trey had found in one of the kitchen drawers, while Christmas carols sounded on the little transistor radio.

Trey shuffled the cards at the end of the latest game. "Are we done?" he asked, stretching his legs under the table. "Everybody had enough?"

"No!" TJ cried, leaning on the table, reaching for his cup of spiced apple cider. "Let's keep playing."

McKenna glanced out the window. Dusk had fallen and it was quickly getting dark. "I need to start the spaghetti sauce soon or we won't eat dinner until late."

"But I'm not hungry yet," TJ said. "And this is fun."

McKenna made a soft sound that sounded an awful lot like a groan. He glanced at her, smiling. "Still having fun?"

She gave him a tortured smile and tugged on her pony-tail, tightening the elastic band. "You know how much I love card games."

Trey laughed softly, enjoying himself, but then, honestly, this was a gift. When he'd learned that McKenna was getting married he'd gone through a hell all of his own and he'd never imagined then, waking up Saturday morning that he'd be here with Mac and TJ today.

This was his Christmas. This was the best gift ever. He honestly couldn't ask for more, and he wasn't ready to think beyond today...and maybe tomorrow.

He and McKenna hadn't talked about the future. As far as he knew, there was no future and maybe once upon a time that would have been hard for him to accept, but four years at Deer Lodge had taught him patience, as well as ac-ceptance.

He couldn't control everything. He couldn't please eve-ryone. He might not be able to please anyone. The only thing he could do, was do his best.

He was trying his best now.

He was focusing on gratitude, too.

Life was short and unpredictable. Instead of going through life feeling entitled, he was going to count his blessings, every single one of them, and right now, his greatest blessings were sitting here at the table playing cards and sipping cider and making him feel like the luckiest man alive.

THE GROUND BEEF and tomato sauce and seasonings were simmering in a pot on the stove and McKenna stepped outside the toasty little kitchen to stand on the porch and watch the white flurries.

Twilight had given way to night. Snow piled high on the porch railing and buried the shrubs by the front of the cabin.

She left the porch and climbed down a step and then another, feeling the snowflakes land on her face and catch in her hair.

It was so quiet out, so blissfully still.

The fresh white snow transformed the landscape, hiding the barren spots, the rocks and dirt, coating weeds so that everything looked beautiful and new.

But wasn't that the magic of Christmas? Wasn't that what made this season so special? Birth, hope, new life…

She glanced over her shoulder back at the cabin and could see through the big picture window Trey and TJ at the table, building a house from the cards. Behind them the fire crackled in the stone hearth and the Christmas tree with the white lights and vintage ornaments cast a colorful glow.

From here on the porch, it looked like a scene from a movie...

If only life was as warm and sweet as a Hallmark movie...

She could use one of those happy endings. TJ, too.

Her eyes burned and she blinked, wanting so badly to give TJ the life she hadn't known. She wanted him to have happiness. She prayed he could grow up without the tragedies she'd experienced. She hoped he could grow from boy to man before he should ever have to suffer and grieve, as she'd suffered and grieved.

It was more than nineteen years since that terrible night when her family had been attacked. And still she couldn't think about it, couldn't picture it, dwell on it, remember in any detail at all how horrific it had been.

Just learning to live without them all had been hard enough. She didn't need to have the horrors burned into her mind.

Trey was such a big part of her healing.

Trey was the one that helped her start to feel safe. Secure.

He was her angel. Her tough, rebel angel.

No one else saw the side she did, but she knew something no one else did—he would protect her with his life.

He would die before he'd let anyone hurt her.

He was there to help her through.

And so when TJ had been conceived, it wasn't this terrible shame, but a gift, and a blessing. TJ was a testament to their love, and proof that good things did happen. Good things would continue to happen.

The cabin door opened and Trey stepped out, gently closing the door, but not shutting it all the way.

"You okay?" he asked, coming down the steps to stand next to her. The snow swirled around him, flakes drifting onto his hair.

She smiled up at him. "Yes."

"You just felt like taking in some snow?"

She crossed her arms over her chest, holding in the emotion. "This has been an amazing day. It's...perfect."

"We didn't really do anything."

"We didn't have to. Just being together made it perfect."

He reached out, and smoothed his hand over the top of her head, and then down the length of her ponytail. "I agree."

He was standing close, very close and she could feel his warmth and his strength. It would be so easy to just lean against him, to absorb his warmth and strength. He'd feel good. He'd feel right. He'd feel like love.

Like home.

She stared up at him, her gaze locking with his, her chest growing heavy, tight.

She wanted him to kiss her.

She wanted him to hold her.

She wanted him to be hers again.

But they'd been down this road before. It hadn't gone well. And the pain of living without Trey when things had gone wrong had been so extreme. The pain was excruciating. It was honestly more than she could bear.

So how did one make it work? How could she love him without constantly worrying, and fearing the worst?

He must have seen her fear and doubts because he clasped her face in his hands, lifting her face to his. His blue eyes "You don't have to know everything, babe. You don't have to solve all the problems of the world tonight. Just live. Just love. Just breathe."

And then his head dropped and his lips covered hers, his lips warm, his breath scented with cinnamon and cider. He kissed her lightly, gently, the pressure just enough to send shivers of pleasure racing up and down her spine.

She reached up, cupping his cheek, fingernails lightly playing against the rough bristles of his beard. He felt so good, his mouth knew hers and she did exactly what he said—she breathed him in, loving him.

It was impossible to be McKenna Douglas without loving Trey Sheenan.

He deepened the kiss, just enough to part her lips, the tip of his tongue tracing the softness of her lower lip and she tingled, growing hot, cold, feeling alive from the top of her head to her tippy toes.

She wanted to tell him she loved him. She wanted to tell

him that she'd never stopped loving him but the words wouldn't come. She was still too afraid of giving him the power to break her heart.

Again.

"Hey, um, Mom." It was TJ in the doorway, and he'd stuck his head outside. "Your spaghetti sauce smells weird on the stove."

Chapter Fourteen

SOMETIME IN THE night it stopped snowing and when they all woke in the morning, the world was a sparkling landscape of frosty white beneath a brilliant blue sky.

TJ and Trey spent the morning sledding and building a snowman before coaxing McKenna out for a massive snowball fight.

It was, as TJ described it, the fight to end all fights, and they ran through the woods, down Cray Road, tramping through knee high powdery snow.

The air was cold and the chill stung McKenna's cheeks but it was also exhilarating racing around lobbing soft snowballs while ducking behind trees.

For a half hour the snowballs flew fast and furious with TJ and Trey joining forces to ambush McKenna. But then TJ changed teams and she and TJ launched a dozen snowballs at Trey, succeeding in getting several well placed ones in his face and collar.

TJ howled with laughter as Trey shook the snow out of

his shirt, and then laughed again as Trey took McKenna down, turning her into a shrieking snow angel.

And then they were all snow angels, lying on their backs beneath the intensely blue sky, moving their arms and legs to create their angel wings.

Chilled from lying in the snow, TJ jumped up and raced to get the sled for one more trip down the hill and Trey gave McKenna a hand, pulling her up to her feet.

"When he stops moving, he's going to be soaked through and cold," McKenna said, watching TJ wrestle with the sled.

"He'll need a hot bath and dry clothes."

"Then lunch, and hopefully a nap."

Trey stretched. "A nap sounds good." He looked down at her and there was heat in his gaze. Desire, too.

She felt herself grow warm even as her heart began to thud, harder, faster.

Awareness licked at her veins, making her belly flip flop.

It would feel amazing to be with him, naked against him, his body filling hers. But the physical would cloud her judgment. The physical would make being rational impossible.

She took a steady step backwards, even as she hoped he'd close the distance and kiss her anyway.

Kiss her again, like he had last night…

Instead he took several steps back, also, and they were now standing a yard or two apart. As if strangers.

She didn't know why she felt a sudden urge to cry. She

didn't know why everything about this moment suddenly felt so deeply unsatisfying.

"This is the Christmas I wanted," he said. "Thank you, Mac."

He sounded sincere but for some reason his sincerity just made her more upset. My pleasure," she said stiffly.

"I've loved every minute I've been able to spend with TJ."

She ground her teeth together. "You said you wanted Christmas with your son. I'm glad you're getting it."

"Not just with him, with you, too."

"Right."

The edge of his mouth lifted. "I mean it."

"Sure. That's why you came to the church to sort out TJ's custody."

"You know it wasn't just about TJ. I was there for you, too."

Her chin jerked up. "It didn't seem that way."

"You were in a wedding gown, marrying someone else. I couldn't exactly storm the church and take you prisoner. There were a hundred and fifty people watching. I had to be careful. Discrete."

She exhaled hard. "You might want to stop talking. Now you're just making me mad."

"Why? Because I've finally grown up enough to realize that what I want and need might not be what you want and need?"

"I'm not sure what you're saying."

He clapped his black gloves, knocking off excess snow. "Let's not do this now."

Her heart felt as if he was about to leap out of her chest. "Do what?"

"Have this conversation. We've had a really fun day, and it's been an incredible Christmas so far—"

"We absolutely do need to have this conversation now. This," she said, jabbing her mitten finger downward, "is exactly what we need to discuss." She stared him in the eye, fierce and furious. And scared. Terribly, terribly scared. "Are you saying you don't want me?"

"That's not what I'm saying."

"Then what *are* you saying?"

"I'm saying…." He drew a breath and yet his expression was firm, and totally unapologetic. "TJ needs us together. *I'd* like us together. But I'm not sure if *us* being together is the best thing for *you*."

She dragged air into her lungs, hating the bittersweet pain that filled her heart. She focused on the wet sheen of icicles lining the edge of the cabin roof to keep from crying or getting even more emotional. "I don't believe you."

His shoulders shifted. "I love you enough to want what's best for you. I'm not sure I'm the best for you."

"Why? What's changed?"

"I have. I know why I love you, and I know what I want for you, and that's for you to be happy. And peaceful. I make you happy some of the time, but together, darlin', we're not peaceful. I don't make you calm and easy. With me, you worry. But I don't want my girl scared and worrying. That's not good for you, not good for us, and not good for our son."

She couldn't believe what she was hearing. And yet, hadn't she just wondered if she could love him? If she could trust him not to hurt her? Not to break her heart again? Did she feel confident in them...or him? "I don't know why you're doing this now."

"I want to protect you."

"Protect me? Or, do you mean, protect yourself? Because my gut is saying you're the coward. My gut is saying you don't want to do the hard work required to make us succeed. My gut thinks you've decided to give up...take the easy way out. That's what I think!"

He gazed at her a long time, eyes flashing fire, but he waited to speak until his tone was calm. Controlled. "I haven't given up on us—I will never give up on us—but we have to be honest and do what is best for each other. Loving me is hard on you, Mac. Loving me hurts you, honey. It took me a long time to get it. Took me those four years in prison to understand what it means to hurt for someone, and baby, I hurt for you. And I hurt for hurting you and I can't ever cause you pain like that again. I couldn't live with myself if I did that."

She turned away to look toward the dark blue lake with

its perimeter of snow frosted trees. It was so pretty...so romantic...and yet there was nothing pretty or romantic about what Trey was saying. "You're killing me," she whispered, reaching up to tug her knit cap down. "You give me hope and then you just take it all away."

"I'm not trying to hurt you. I'm trying to protect you from future pain—"

"The future isn't here! There's nothing here but you and me and TJ. So Sheenan, don't you dare say you're being practical and honest and all mature, because guess what? You're not that practical and mature. You came to my wedding Saturday, you interrupted the service, you took TJ and then you grabbed me, stealing us from the church. You kidnapped me on my wedding day. And you didn't turn around, you didn't go back, and you didn't feel remorse. You dragged us to a diner for a wedding night dinner and somehow between Marietta and White Sulphur Springs you captured TJ's heart, and melted mine, and sorry, but you can't act all good and chivalrous now, because it's too late! You're not this great guy. You're not selfless and you're not altruistic and your love is demanding and fierce and you do want me. You still want me, you bastard, and don't you ever say you don't!"

She shoved her mitten across her face, wiping her eyes, swiping at her nose. "Don't you ever," she repeated thickly. "Because it's not fair. Not when we both know what we've always known—we were made for each other. We are meant to be together. And that's why we have a son together. He's not an accident. We are not an accident. And I'm tired of living like we—this—us—is just one colossal mistake!"

She marched back to the cabin, desperate to get inside before TJ saw her cry.

Damn him.

Damn Trey.

He was the worst, most awful man in the world.

And if he was her angel, he was a fallen angel and it'd fallen on her to save his ass.

TREY SAT IN one of the chairs by the fire, cleaning the snowshoes he'd found in the shed. The wood frames still looked good but the rawhide lacings were worn and needed attention. It seemed that mice had gotten to the leather and he made a note to order new lacings once he returned to Marietta. In the meantime, he carefully rubbed the ash frames dry, grateful to have something to occupy his hands and attention.

Dinner had been on the quiet side, at least between himself and McKenna. TJ had talked up a storm and hadn't seem to notice, and once the dishes were done, McKenna curled up with TJ on the little couch, making up stories and asking TJ what he thought Santa Claus was doing right now.

She was still mad at him, still not talking to him, while showering TJ with hugs and kisses.

He didn't mind McKenna showering TJ with love.

McKenna should be an affectionate Mom. She should tell stories and play and be fun.

But Trey was having a hard time being shut out from the fun. He struggled with McKenna punishing him for being a *bad* guy, when in this instance, he was the *good* guy.

He hadn't spent four years missing her and picturing a future with her, a future that hopefully included more children and family trips and holidays and traditions, to let go so easily. It was a life he wanted with every bit of his being...but it had to be right. For both of them. Otherwise it wasn't the family life either of them desired.

He didn't want a resentful or anxious wife. He didn't want to be the source of someone's anger, or worry.

He was who he was, and he was trying damn hard to do things better, but he'd never do everything perfectly. He'd make mistakes. He'd be impulsive, using his heart before his head. But that was who he was. He wasn't Troy. Or Brock. Dillon or Cormac. He was himself.

Not bad.

Just not perfect.

Which was why he was trying to think of *her*, and what *she* needed. McKenna had been through a lot in her life. They never talked about what happened at the Douglas Ranch that one night, but he'd read about it in the papers. The murders had been discussed in agonizing detail around town. Trey's dad had been one of the first responders on the scene, as the Sheenan ranch lay close to the Douglas property, but he wouldn't talk about what he'd seen at the Douglas ranch, other than the thing he'd said when he came home: *it was the worst, most violent scene imaginable, and if God had any mercy at all, he'd let that one poor boy survive.*

Trey glanced up from the snowshoes to McKenna, watching her whisper something playful into TJ's ear and making TJ giggle.

She deserved to be happy.

They all deserved to be happy.

Which didn't mean he was walking away from her, or giving up on her, or giving up on them.

It just meant they had to be mature, and patient. They had to talk, and listen, and get a hell of a lot better at communicating.

They nailed some parts of it. They were experts at hot sex. But now they needed to get good at the other things, working together to make sure their relationship would last. He wanted what his parents didn't have. A happy marriage.

A true partnership.

And you only got that with respect, trust, faith, forgiveness.

McKenna HAD FORGOTTEN that when Trey was hurt he grew quiet. She'd forgotten that he wasn't loud and out of control, but silent and thoughtful. Reserved.

He was certainly reserved now. He'd shut down, retreating to a chair in the corner where he sat doing manly chores and repairs, like weatherproof the old wooden snowshoes.

She wasn't trying to ignore him, but she wasn't going to struggle to fill the silence with meaningless small talk, either.

However, once TJ fell asleep on her lap, worn out from sledding and snowball fights and tramping around in the snow, the living room, silent except for the crackle and pop of the fire, felt uncomfortable.

Tomorrow was Christmas Eve. This wasn't how she wanted Christmas to be.

She didn't even know what had happened outside, earlier. Everything just seemed to shift and tilt and go wildly wrong.

She felt an ache as she watched Trey work, his dark head bent.

She wanted things different. She wanted them better. She wanted more with Trey, not less.

Not this.

Silence and anger and hurt.

Suddenly his head lifted and he looked up at her, his brow furrowed, expression shuttered. "If I didn't want what was best for you, Mac, I'd be no man at all."

"But who are you to decide what's best for me?" she retorted defiantly. "Who are you to tell me what I need?"

"I know what you need. I've known you too long not to know. And for the record, I never said we're finished, never said we're through, because God as my witness, I will never ever walk away from you. I will always want you. I will always love you. And we might fight, and we might disagree, but that doesn't mean I'm abandoning you. You're my girl. But I've got to do right by you."

"Then love me."

"I do."

"And don't say we can't make it work—"

"Never said that."

"And don't imply that you're the wrong guy, or that there might be a better guy. Whether there is, or isn't, is a moot point, because I want you. I choose you." She drew an unsteady breath. "I love you."

There was just silence for a moment, but it wasn't the silence of before. This was soft and full...warm and hopeful.

"That's why I climbed in the truck with you and TJ," she added quietly. "I wasn't being kidnapped. I wasn't being forced anywhere. I wanted to go with you...I wanted to be with you. I've wanted to be with you since I was fifteen and thought you were my very own knight in tarnished armor."

Creases fanned from his eyes. The corners of his mouth tilted. "Tarnished armor, hmm?"

She could see him back as they were in high school. She remembered how he'd avoided her all Fall of her freshman year, even though she knew he was aware of her. She knew he knew she was there. And she didn't know why he kept his distance, but as the weeks passed, September to October, and then October to November, she didn't want him to keep his distance. She wanted him close, talking to her, close, dancing with her, close, kissing her.

She just wanted him close.

She just wanted him. Not sexually—she wasn't that mature, or precocious—but she craved his company and wanted to look into his blue eyes and see if she could see more, see deeper. She wanted to look until she was full, look until her heart was overflowing.

"I chose you a long time ago," she added, voice dropping to a whisper. "And we've had some hard years. Now we just have to figure out how to make this work."

THEY MADE LOVE in the four poster log bed in the master bedroom, beneath the heavy handmade quilts, with the snow stacked on the windowsill, blocking out much of the moon light.

They'd waited years to come together, years to be one, and the lovemaking was slow and hushed, breath catching, lips touching, hands skimming. Trey took his time kissing her, kissing everywhere, enjoying the satin and silk of her skin, the warmth of her body, the curves that were uniquely hers. He breathed her in, the heat, the taste, the scent and he loved her so much, so deeply, that in some ways he didn't know where he ended and she began.

She was that much a part of him and his heart.

For the first time in a long long time, McKenna felt completely safe. Completely at peace.

She was lying in the circle of Trey's arms, her cheek

against his chest. She could hear his heart. She could feel his strength, his power deceptive when he was relaxed.

He shifted, rolling her over onto her back to look down into her face. "I want to marry you," he said. "I want TJ to have us, both of us together. A real family. He deserves that. We deserve that."

"Are you proposing, Sheenan?"

His lips curved but his expression was fierce, intense. "We were engaged the last time I saw you."

She swallowed, nodded. True. "I still have the ring. It's at the bank, in a safe. I didn't want anything to happen to it."

"Speaking of rings, where is Lawrence's? I haven't seen you wear it since we left White Sulphur Springs."

"It's tucked away to return it to him once I'm back in Marietta." She reached up to touch his cheek, her fingertips sliding over his cheekbone and then down along the hard chiseled jaw. "You know that I haven't done this since you left, four years ago. There's been no one but you. Ever."

He frowned. "You and Lawrence...?"

She shook her head. "We agreed to wait until we were married. I think he thought I was virtuous. I wasn't virtuous. I just wasn't...eager. It was easy to wait."

"How could you marry him then?"

"I was trying so hard to get over you. Trying so hard to build a life without you." She gulped a breath. "Thank God you arrived when you did. If you hadn't..." Her voice drifted away, her insides lurching. "It wouldn't have been good."

"Then we need to make this good. We need to be good." He turned his face into her hand, kissing her palm. "We can't be hotheads anymore. Can't be brash or impulsive."

"You're the impulsive one," she countered. "You're the one that leaps before looking."

His lips curved. "Maybe."

"Don't be brash anymore. Don't be stupid."

"Ouch." But he was smiling.

She smiled back, even as she wound her arms around his neck. "Be smart. Be safe. Be mine, forever."

"I am, babe. Forever and ever."

Chapter Fifteen

T J WOKE FIRST. It was early, almost ungodly early as he shouted from the living room. "Santa came! Santa was here!"

McKenna quickly pulled her night shirt on and left the warm bed to shiver in the middle of the room. "Come on, Santa, you need to build a fire. I'll get the coffee brewing."

In the living room TJ was crouched by the Christmas tree studying the colorful packages that magically appeared in the night.

"Are any of these for me?" he asked, touching the gifts and trying to read names on the tags.

"I think most of them are for you," she answered, smiling as she buttoned up the oversized Salish knit cardigan she'd turned into her robe. "Santa must think you've been a very good boy."

"But someone wasn't good," TJ said, pointing to the row of stockings hanging from the stone fireplace. "One of them has black stuff in it."

"Coal."

TJ looked worried. "That's *bad*."

Yawning Trey entered the room and glanced up at the three stockings hanging from the stone mantle. Two red and green and cream stockings, and one green and white one. "Which is mine?" he asked.

"I hope you didn't get the one with coal," TJ said.

Trey glanced from the stockings to McKenna, an eyebrow rising. "Bad, huh?"

She shrugged. "It's from Santa. He keeps the list, naughty and nice." Then she crossed to his side, and leaned down to whisper. "Although last night I think you were both naughty and nice."

His blue gaze warmed. "Very very nice."

"Or, very very bad..."

"Which can also be nice."

She blushed and kissed him before straightening. "I'm going to make coffee.

You guys build the fire and then we'll have to see what Santa brought everyone."

TJ LOVED HIS gifts, all of them, letting out delighted squeals every time he opened a new presents. He tore through the paper, destroying ribbons and careful wrap to crow with pleasure as he discovered the gift.

Boxes of Lego. The set of tin soldiers. A football. A Mine Craft backpack. Matchbox cars and a figure 8 track for the cars to race on.

TJ wanted to play with everything right away but then settled down with the tin soldiers, setting up two army camps on the floor by the tree.

McKenna went to make breakfast, eggs and hash brown and cinnamon coffee cake. She'd just slid the coffee cake into the oven when Trey came to the kitchen. "I have one more gift," he said, holding out a small box with an enormous red bow. "I found it in a little art and crafts gallery in Cherry Lake. It reminded me of you."

She put the pot holders down and took the little box with the huge crimson silk ribbon. It was so pretty. The ribbon itself was a work of art. "I don't have anything else for you," she said regretfully. "Just that Pendleton shirt I gave you earlier."

"I like my shirt. I haven't had a new shirt in a while."

"I would have shopped more but I was using your money. It didn't feel right buying you presents with your own money."

"Now that's not entirely true. You did give me something else. A very nice gift, full of tender loving thoughts." His dark head inclined. "Thank you for that wonderful sock full of coal."

She laughed, her expression mischievous. "I couldn't help it. The stocking *screamed* your name."

"I'm sure it did." His lips were still quirked and then his smile faded but his expression was infinitely warm. "And this one, Mac, screamed yours."

She tugged off the ribbon and removed the paper and lifted the lid. Inside the delicate tissue paper was a necklace. An angel hanging from a gold necklace.

And the angel looked like a miniature version of the angel ornaments she'd sold him all those years ago.

"You know what this looks like," she said.

"The dozen brass angels I bought from you."

"Yes." She lifted the angel, studying it more closely, the chain sliding through her fingers. "Is this a sapphire?"

"A Montana sapphire."

"I love it so much." She leaned forward and kissed him, and kissed him again. "I love you so much."

"I know you do."

"We're going to make this work, Trey. We're going to get it right this time."

"That's the plan."

"No craziness. Just family and work and love." She smiled into his eyes. "Lots and lots of love."

"Sounds perfect." He took the necklace from her, opened the clasp, waiting while she lifted her long hair and then fastened it around her neck.

She turned back around to face him. "How does it look?" she asked, touching the angel which hit just at her breastbone.

"Beautiful."

"Thank you."

"My pleasure." He hesitated. "Speaking of family and work and love…have you thought about where you want to live?"

She hesitated, her fingers rubbing across the angel and stone. "I would have thought you'd want to live on the Sheenan ranch."

"But I know the idea of living on the ranch makes you nervous," he said.

She said nothing, her gaze clinging to his.

"And yes, the ranch house is big enough. It has what? Five bedrooms? But it's not the space that has you worried. It's the fact that we're so remote."

"Yes."

"I think TJ would love living on the ranch. The horses, the dogs. All the space to play."

"I loved living on our ranch, until…" Her voice faded and she hung her head, rubbing the angel again, needing courage, and comfort. "But if it's what you wanted for TJ, if it's that important to you, we could try. I could…try."

"But you'd be scared."

She nodded.

"Even with me there," he added.

She nodded again. "I'm sorry."

He reached for her, drawing her against him, his hands looping low on her back. "Don't be sorry. I don't blame you for being frightened. If I were you, I'd be nervous, too."

She exhaled slowly. This had been a sticking point for

them, years ago. Trey had wanted to live on the ranch. She had wanted to live in town. He couldn't run the ranch from town but she couldn't imagine living so isolated. What if something bad happened again? What if...?

She swallowed hard. "My fear is irrational, I know that. And Sheenans are ranchers, I know that, too. But I really really don't want to be way out there, especially if you're not at the house, and let's face it, you'll be out working on the ranch, taking care of the cattle and the property, not hanging around the kitchen."

"So we live in town."

"And the ranch?"

"We'll figure that out."

"What does that mean?"

"It means the ranch isn't half as important as you, and your peace of mind. Maybe Dillon will want to run it. Maybe I'll sell it—"

"Trey, no!"

"I've lived without the ranch for the past four years, and I was fine. But I wasn't fine living without you." His gaze was steady, his expression somber as he reached up to move a loose tendril of hair from her brow. His fingers were gentle, his touch sure. "A job is a job, but family is forever."

His tenderness made her chest ache. "And yet since I've met you, you've only wanted one thing—to run the Sheenan ranch one day."

"Two things," he corrected. "You and the ranch, but as I

said, I didn't burn and ache for the ranch at Deer Lodge, but honey, I burned and ached for you."

THEY HAD A leisurely breakfast and then Trey and TJ washed up the dishes so McKenna could take a bath and sample some of the bubbles and body wash and scented shampoo Trey had filled her stocking with.

McKenna sighed with pleasure as she soaked in the hot tub, the vanilla and nutmeg scented bubbles tickling her chin.

It had been a great day...a great few days. Christmas this year had been so joyous...an absolute miracle.

She reached up to touch the angel on her necklace, her fingers rubbing at the gold figure holding the sapphire hearth.

Just as Trey was her miracle.

And her angel.

AFTER MCKENNA'S BATH it was TJ's turn, and then he and Trey built one of his Lego sets and McKenna made an early lunch, serving the grilled cheese sandwiches and tomato soup with an apology for it not being more festive.

Neither of the boys seemed to mind but when Trey cleared the lunch dishes, bringing them into the kitchen, McKenna was already worrying about Christmas dinner. "What about tonight?" she asked. "I don't have a roast or turkey, nothing special for a proper Christmas dinner. Do you think there is anything open today...we could buy something, or make reservations somewhere?"

"We don't need anything fancy," Trey answered, scraping the plates and rinsing the soup bowls. "TJ doesn't care about what we eat, and trust me, I'm not picky, either."

"But it's Christmas. Christmas should be extra special. Food, festivities, family."

He turned off the water, faced her. "We could go back to Marietta. If we leave in the next hour we'd be able to join everyone gathering at Brock and Harley's for Christmas dinner. They're hosting the family this year. Most of the Sheenans will be there...Troy and Taylor. Dillon. Possibly Cormac, but with Daisy he's not a given."

"Can we do that? Just show up uninvited?"

"I'm a Sheenan. I'm always invited, and there will be plenty to eat. Apparently Harley's from a big Dutch family and always cooks enough to feed an army." He reached for her, pulling her against him. "But we don't have to go. It's only if you want to. I don't want there to be any pressure or worries on Christmas Day."

She glanced behind her, over at TJ who'd returned to playing with his new Star Wars Lego figurines, delighted by the Storm Troopers. "Aren't they going to think it's strange, you showing up with us on Christmas when they know less than a week ago I was supposed to marry Lawrence?"

"I think they'd think it was strange if I didn't show up with you and TJ. I'm pretty sure they're rooting for us, hoping we can work it out."

"But they're not going to expect a big formal announcement, are they? I mean, you and I are still trying to figure it out."

He smiled and lightly rubbed at the worry line between her brows. "I can assure you there's no pressure in that direction. I think you know we Sheenans tend to operate under a Hope-for-the-best-but-prepare-for-the-worst scenario."

She made a face. "Or at least they do with you."

"As they should," he teased.

She glanced out the window at the blue sky and sparkling drifts of powdery white snow with the dark blue of the lake shimmering in the background before letting her gaze skim the interior of the cabin. "You think we can take down the tree and empty the cupboards and strip all the beds in an hour?" Her nose wrinkled. "It doesn't sound like a festive way to spend the morning."

"Let's just unplug the tree and toss out the perishables and then I'll just come back after New Year's with the new generator and get that installed and deal with everything else."

"That's a lot of work for one person."

Trey's laughter rumbled from his chest. "Darlin', I've just spent four years at Deer Lodge. Tidying up a cabin and taking a tree down is not hard work. Besides, I like it here, and I'd love to get that generator replaced so we can get all the Sheenans here and enjoy it as a family."

MCKENNA MOVED AS much of the food from the refrigerator to the freezer and tossed what wouldn't last a week or two and then turned her attention to making the beds since they weren't going to strip the sheets.

Trey unplugged the tree, put out the fire, and turned off the heater before crouching next to TJ to help him gather up the new toys and put them in TJ's new black and green Mine Craft backpack. McKenna smiled as TJ made decisions about which pockets would get which toys—some for the Legos, some for the miniature tin soldiers, and some for the Christmas taffy and treats.

"I wish we didn't have to go," he said mournfully, as the new suitcase, filled with all their new clothes, was carried out to the truck.

"We'll be back," Trey said, rifling TJ's dark hair. "Not just this winter, but in the spring and summer. We'll get a boat and go out on the lake. We can fish and have camp fires and make s'mores. It'll be fun."

McKenna understood TJ's wistfulness. She had mixed feelings about leaving, too. These past few days had felt special…magical…and she wasn't sure she was ready to leave the safety and quiet of the cabin at Cherry Lake for 'real life' in Marietta.

Back in Marietta they'd get drawn into work and school and be subjected to everyone's opinions.

She didn't want everyone's opinion. She didn't want to be lectured or fussed over, or have well meaning family and friends give her 'advice'. She didn't want the gossip, either, and there would be plenty of gossip.

It wasn't that she couldn't handle the gossip—good grief, she'd been surrounded by it for most of her life—but she dreaded having TJ exposed to it. And she hated knowing that Trey would be at the center of it.

That bad Trey Sheenan was back...

Trey was home and already causing trouble...

He climbed the steps of the cabin and stood before her, arms crossed over his broad chest. "What's wrong?"

She managed a smile. "Nothing. Why?"

"Mac, I know you, babe. I know your face. I know your sighs. I know when something is on your mind. What is it? Don't want to do Christmas with my family? We don't have to—"

"This isn't about your family. I like your family, and I know they like me, and absolutely adore TJ..." She looked up into his face, searching his eyes, not wanting secrets between them but also unwilling to hurt him. "It's about you. I'm worried what people will say about you." She swallowed hard. "And me, us. But mostly, about you. They've never been kind to you—"

"Because I've never earned their respect," he interrupted flatly. "I'm not going back to Marietta expecting anyone to be a fan, or a friend. I don't need anyone's approval. But I hope their criticism doesn't extend to TJ. He might have my name, but he's not me. He's his own little person and a really good little person." His voice cracked and he looked away, jaw tightening and flexing as his gaze fell on TJ who was poking holes in the snow with a stick. "I don't mind if they hit me, and hate me. But they have to leave him alone."

McKenna fought tears as she wrapped her arms around Trey and hugged him, hard, harder. "He's a tough little boy. He's got the best of both of us, and a big family that will always have his back...the Sheenans and the Douglasses, two of the oldest, strongest families in Crawford County. You can't ask for more than that."

IN THE TRUCK as they pulled away, McKenna turned to get a last glance at the cabin. It was a true cabin, small and sturdy and simple, without luxurious bells and whistles, which was why it was so perfect.

They'd had no TV or computer games. Just Christmas carols on the radio, and the one NPR personality that read the stories on Christmas Eve.

It was an old fashioned Christmas, small and cozy with just the right amount of presents and surprises and holiday cheer.

It'd be easy to stay here and hide from life in Marietta, but their life was in Marietta and it had to be faced, sooner or later.

Maybe it was better it was happening sooner.

Maybe the best thing was just to face the haters and critics head on, and work their way through it.

Eventually the gossip would die down. Eventually the town would find someone new, or something else shocking, to whisper about.

She'd be glad when they did. Not that she wished trouble or small town gossip on anyone.

With the recent heavy snow fall Highway 83 would be too treacherous, if the mountain pass was even open, so Trey turned left onto 93, heading for Polson, and then they'd hit I-90 which would lead them straight to Bozeman and on to the junction of Highway 89.

But even the road along the lake was slick, and she was glad it was Trey at the wheel. He was far better with ice than she.

They were just a few miles from the cabin when they rounded a corner and deep tire marks sliced sideways through snow and ice, a diagonal slash across the road that stretched all the way to the embankment overlooking the lake. The skid of the tires looked perfectly fresh. The accident must have just happened.

"Oh no," McKenna said, leaning forward. "Look," she added, pointing to the group forming at the lake.

Trey pulled over, shifted into park and jumped out. McKenna told TJ to stay put and jumped out, too.

A small white car was parked haphazardly on the side of the road, and a motorcycle stood abandoned there as well.

People were on phones. Someone else was shouting for rope.

"The woman lost control and her car went into the lake," one of the female bystanders cried into her phone, almost hysterical. "Hurry! She had a baby in her car. They're under water."

People were shouting, cars continued to pull over. It was pure chaos. Trey glanced at McKenna for a split second—if that—but the Trey she knew was gone. The other Trey was here. The one who shut down emotions, the one who deadened feelings. The impulsive, reckless devil-take-all Trey.

Her heart fell. "Trey!"

But he was already gone, skidding down the icy embankment to the water's edge. A man stood next to the lake, his clothing soaked to his waist, dripping icy water onto the packed snow. "I couldn't get to her, man. I can't even see the car. The water is freezing and dark."

"How many people in the car?" Trey asked, stripping off his heavy jacket.

"Two, three. A lady and a baby. Don't know if there was more, but I saw the car seat. There was a car seat. I was right behind her when she swerved and went in."

Trey dove in.

THERE WERE MOMENTS engraved in one's memory, moments that became memories, both wonderful and horrifying.

The time Trey spent underwater was endless. The actual time could have been seconds, minutes, but it felt like a lifetime.

McKenna saw a lifetime of memories and moments with him. In high school. After school. Working. Loving. Fighting. Conceiving TJ. Struggling. Loving. Missing. Suffering.

Life with Trey could be difficult, but life without him was impossible.

Life without him wasn't like living at all.

And this—this thing he was doing—was exactly what she feared most. She hated the reckless dangerous Trey. Hated that he had so little regard for his own life. Hated that he could just abandon her and TJ without a second thought...second glance...

Hated that the one person she needed most, didn't need her the same way.

If he loved them, he wouldn't jeopardize his family...

But in the very same moment she knew that he did what he did, took these incredible risks, because he had heart.

His strength was a gift.

His courage set him apart.

He was brave and foolhardy, but weren't all protectors that way?

In that moment where she thought she'd lost him forever, swallowed by the icy cold lake, she understood him best, and what happened that day at the Wolf Den.

A man was putting his fist in a woman's face.

A girl disappeared in a fast-flowing river, and no one realized it was serious until too late.

A car went into a freezing lake with a mother and child inside.

Trey couldn't stand idly by. Trey couldn't look the other way. Trey was not a bystander, and he'd never do nothing if he could do *something*.

Even if it meant he lost everything he loved.

He risked all, because he knew what it was to love.

And then he was up, dragging a woman to the surface. People rushed forward to take the woman and then Trey was gone again, diving back under.

HELP CAME RUSHING in, in the form of a helicopter from Kalispell Regional Medical Center, the helicopter landing on the closed highway, sheriffs and fire trucks now blocking the road to keep the area clear.

McKenna stood with TJ, shivering uncontrollably while the helicopter slowly rose, blades whirring, blowing snow as the helicopter airlifted the mother, the baby and Trey out together. The paramedics had told McKenna she'd have to follow in the truck as there was no room in the chopper, and she understood, but at the same time she was shaking so badly she couldn't drive quite yet.

Her emotions had run the gamut from fear to joy, and

she felt worked…wrecked.

Trey surfacing the second time, with the toddler, had been beyond wonderful. The crowd lining the road had cheered. But then Trey lost consciousness and the local fire station medics rushed in and hauled him out of the water, and seeing Trey carried from the water, head hanging, body limp had been terrifying.

She'd thought they'd lost him.

She thought *she'd* lost him.

For a second, she couldn't breathe, couldn't get air. For a second, it felt like her heart had stopped.

"Do you want to use that phone now?" One of the ladies on the side of the road asked, holding her cell phone to McKenna.

McKenna stared at her blankly.

"You said you didn't have a phone, and you needed to make a call?" The woman's reminder was gentle. But then, people had been so kind, moved by Trey's actions, impressed by his courage and selflessness.

McKenna's hand shook as she punched in Paige's number. Thankfully Paige answered. "Merry Christmas, McKenna! Where are you? How are you? How's—"

"There's been an accident," McKenna choked, her throat constricting. "I'm over at Flathead Lake. I've been staying at the Sheenan family cabin outside Cherry Lake. Trey's hurt. He's being airlifted to the Kalispell hospital right now. Can you please alert his family? If Troy's not at the Graff, he'll probably be at Brock and Harley's."

"I'm on it."

"Thank you."

"Are you okay?"

McKenna reached up to touch the angel hanging from her neck. "Only if he is."

"He will be, McKenna. He's strong. He's Trey."

"I'm trying to remember that."

Chapter Sixteen

TREY WOKE UP slowly, thoughts thick and tangled, his body heavy and sore. Had he been drinking? Had he been fighting?

He glanced around. Everything was beige and bland. Sterile.

He tried to sit up but something tugged in his forearm. He reached over, fingers skimming the tape and tubing. His confusion increased.

Where was he, and what the hell was going on?

Where was McKenna? And TJ? Why weren't they here—where had he left them? Lost them?

And then pictures flashed, and it started to come back to him: the crowd at the lake, the tire marks that led from the road to the lake, and someone screaming about a lady and her kids.

He didn't remember pulling over. He didn't remember jumping out. He did remember looking at McKenna, briefly. He didn't remember what she said, or if she said anything, but he saw her eyes, saw her terror.

But he must have gone into the lake, because he remembered it was cold, shockingly cold, like a knife plunging into his lungs.

But he swam down. He swam for the submerged car and he dragged a lady up, and out. And then numb, he went down again.

It wasn't that dark down below, though, just terribly cold, and he shoved into the back of the car, wrestled with the buckles and harness on a car seat. The child wasn't moving. The child was still but Trey wouldn't think about that. He wouldn't think about anything but getting the child out, and then up.

Up.

Up.

Sunlight. Air.

"Hey, Baby." A quiet voice sounded at his side. Hands touched him, one hand on his arm, the other on his chest. "You're awake." And then McKenna was leaning over him, kissing his forehead and then his cheek. "Merry Christmas."

He struggled to focus on her face, and then she was clear, and beautiful, so very very beautiful. "Where's TJ?"

"With Troy."

"Troy's here?"

"Everybody's here. Well, everybody but Cormac, but Dillon said he might be coming."

"Why?"

"To spend Christmas together. As a family."

He was silent for awhile, processing, even as he felt the icy cold water all over again, remembered the bone chilling shock of it. "The baby in the car seat…is he…did he…?"

"She. She's a twenty-two month old girl, and she's been airlifted to Missoula, but from all reports, she's stable and the doctors are predicting a full recovery."

"Are you just saying that?"

"No. You can ask Brock or Troy. They've talked to the medical team at the Children's Hospital. You saved her. You saved both of them, the mother and the daughter." McKenna's eyes filled with tears. "You are a hero."

"Not a hero. Never been a hero—"

"You've always been my hero, even if you don't keep your armor all shiny and silver." She leaned over and kissed him carefully. "But you did scare me, babe. I thought I lost you."

He reached up and caught one of her tears. "Is that why you're crying?"

"I'm crying because I'm lucky. I'm blessed. You're a good man. You're tough and strong…absolutely fearless."

"Oh, Mac, not fearless. I was terrified."

"But you went after them anyway. There were others standing there. That man was standing there. They didn't go in. They were waiting for help to arrive."

"There was no time," Trey said. "I had to do it. Someone had to do it."

Her tears kept falling, and he couldn't stop them. His chest tightened, his heart hurting because he'd hurt her again. "I scared you," he whispered.

"You did," she agreed, drawing a rough breath. "And I could have lost you. For a while there, I wondered if we had. But I suddenly understood you, while you were down there, I suddenly understood why I love you. It's because you are a protector. And the world needs tough men, risk-taking men, men like you. And I hope and pray that when TJ grows up, he'll end up just like you. Flawed but perfect. Trey Sheenan, you have no idea how much I love you."

TREY WAS RELEASED late afternoon the next day from the Medical Center in Kalispell. McKenna was there to pick him up in Troy's big black SUV as Troy had insisted it was safer and more comfortable than Trey's old truck.

It was almost dark by the time they reached Cherry Lake and the drive up Cray Road still had lots of snow but the parking area by the cabin had been shoveled clear. "Who did this?" Trey asked.

"Your brothers," she answered, pulling into an empty spot and shifting into park.

"Why? Did they think I was coming home in a wheel-chair?"

"I think they needed something to do." She turned off the engine and gave him a level look. "They were worried sick about you."

"Sounds like I did a good job of ruining Christmas."

"Hardly. Your brothers are like big kids. They've been having the time of their life, playing with the real kids." She saw his expression and added. "Mack and Molly are awesome with TJ, very sweet, incredibly patient. It's been good for everyone to be here as a family—"

"Where's everyone sleeping?"

"Dillon's on the couch. Brock, Harley and the twins are in the loft. Troy and Taylor have taken the guest room with the twin beds, and TJ and I are in the master bedroom, waiting for you to return."

"You sound pretty smug." But he was smiling as he said it, his expression gentle.

"Not smug, just happy." She leaned over and kissed him. "And it might sound corny, but I think your mom's here...at least, her spirit is here. There is so much love in that house...so much good will. I think she needed this, here, having all her boys on Cray land, in the Cray cabin."

"Not all. We're missing Cormac."

"He said he'd try to come. He was working on a flight."

"It's a long haul from Southern California—" he broke off as the sound of an engine pierced the quiet, and a big pewter colored SUV roared up the road and into the driveway.

Trey and McKenna looked at the driver and then looked at each other and smiled.

Cormac was here. He'd made it.

You wouldn't know it was December 26th. It felt like Christmas Day.

Trey sat in the chair by the fire with TJ on his lap and McKenna on the floor at his feet, leaning back against his knee.

The Sheenans filled the small cabin, talking, laughing, sharing memories of Christmases past.

Trey enjoyed listening to his brothers tease and argue. They were as always—intense, competitive, boisterous, but ultimately loving.

It wasn't an easy family but it was his family, and he was grateful he had a son who would carry on the Sheenan name.

Just then Troy appeared with plastic red cups half filled with cold fizzy champagne. "Where did you get the champagne from?" Brock asked, wagging his finger at his twins, letting them know they wouldn't be drinking.

"Taylor and I picked up a couple bottles in town today, to celebrate Trey's return home, and our first Christmas together in years." Troy passed out the remaining cups so that all the adults had one. "If Trey hadn't played hero, this wouldn't have happened—"

"Not a hero," Trey protested gruffly.

"You are to us," Cormac said, from where he stood next to the tree with three year old Daisy in his arms.

"You are to *me*," Dillon added quietly.

"And me," TJ said, sitting up, looking around. "You saved a mom and a baby. That's like...well, being a superhero."

Brock smiled faintly. "Trey, our Superhero."

"Ha!" Trey protested, flushing and squirming a little, undone by the support. To have his family here, accepting him, including him, meant more than he could say.

"So I propose a toast," Troy said, lifting his red cup. "To Trey who helped bring us together this year. It's so good to have you home."

"To Trey!" they all cheered, and then drank.

The champagne was cold and crisp, and the bubbles fizzed, making Trey smile. The cabin might be small and rustic, and the champagne might be served in plastic cups, but this was one of the most festive Christmases he could remember.

Trey lifted his cup. "I have a toast, too." He glanced around the room, at his brothers, Harley, Taylor, the kids. His son. McKenna. And suddenly he wasn't sure he'd be able to make the toast. Suddenly he felt so much emotion he couldn't speak.

But then he felt a calm, and a peace, and he took a breath and tried to put his gratitude into words. "To Dad and Mom," he said, his deep voice cracking. "May we remember the best in them, and cherish the good, and may we forget the pain and hurts and forgive so that only the love remains."

The room was silent and for a moment Trey wondered if he'd said too much, maybe said the wrong thing. Then he felt McKenna squeeze his knee and Cormac raised his cup. "Beautifully said. To Mom and Dad."

"Mom and Dad," everyone echoed. "To the Sheenans and the Crays."

They stayed up late into the night talking and laughing and sharing stories as well as planning weddings. Troy and Taylor were still discussing a Valentine's wedding but it looked as if there would be a wedding much sooner.

Trey and McKenna wanted a barn wedding on the Sheenan property on New Year's Eve. McKenna joked that she'd take her wedding dress and cut it off at the knees and top it with the red flannel shirt tied at the waist.

"All you'd need would be some red cowboy boots," Troy said. "And I'm pretty sure you have a pair."

"No veil," Trey said. "You have to leave your hair down."

"And you, Trey, would have to come in all black," McKenna retorted. "Only appropriate if we're re-enacting the great wedding escape."

Harley glanced from Trey to TJ. "Are you two serious?"

Trey and McKenna's gazes locked and held. He was the first to smile. "I'd marry her today," he said slowly, blue eyes gleaming, "but we need a license."

"And the ring," she added, lips twitching. "It's in Marietta in a safe deposit box."

"But the barn will be cold," Harley said with mock sternness. "It's not an appropriate barn for weddings."

"And it'll smell," Taylor added. Maybe we can see if the Emerson Barn is free."

Harley nodded and reached for her smart phone, doing a quick search and then checking an online calendar. "I'm on their website events page now. The barn is booked for the 31st, for a large private New Year's Eve party, but it is open on the 30th and on the evening of New Year's Day."

She looked expectantly at Trey and McKenna. "Should we make a reservation request?"

"It's a huge barn and there's only a few of us," McKenna protested.

"You have to invite your brothers," Trey said. "And sweet Aunt Karen."

McKenna rolled her eyes at the sweet Aunt Karen part, but Trey was right. She couldn't get married without her brothers and Aunt Karen there. They'd never forgive her. "Paige, too. And her kids. Plus Jenny and Colton Thorpe."

"Sage and Callan Carrigan," someone said.

"Well, Callan for sure," Dillon answered. "If you want all the family there."

The conversation abruptly died. Heads turned, eyes on Dillon.

Brock was the first to speak, his dark brows flat over intense dark eyes. "That was odd," he said carefully. "Want to repeat that?"

Dillon didn't immediately answer. Seconds passed and the tension grew. Finally he shrugged. "We have a lot to talk about."

More silence followed.

Trey and Troy exchanged swift glances.

Cormac frowned. "Does anybody know what's going on?"

"A little bit," Troy admitted. "But I think Dillon knows more than the rest of us."

"I do," Dillon agreed. "But I don't think this is the time, not with the kids here, not when we're supposed to be enjoying each other's company."

"It's that bad," Trey said flatly.

"Or...good...depending on how you look at it."

No one looked reassured.

"I think you're right about tonight not being the time or place," Troy said. "Not just because of the kids, but because this is the Cray cabin. This is Mom's place."

IT WAS WELL after midnight when everyone had turned in and the cabin lights turned off. In the master bedroom it was Trey and McKenna with TJ in the middle.

TJ had fallen asleep hours ago and Trey and McKenna held hands, their linked fingers resting on his hip.

"What do you think of your Christmas?" McKenna whispered in the dark.

"I think it was the best Christmas ever."

"Because everybody was here?"

"Because Christmas this year was a whole week long."

"How do you figure that?"

"Day 1, kidnapping you and TJ from the church."

"You can't celebrate that."

"Of course I can. Day 2, Explore Cherry Lake. Day 3, movie and Christmas shopping. Day 4, snow fun. Day 5, Christmas Eve. Day 6, Christmas. Day 7, everybody here with us."

She smiled in the dark. "That does sound like a lovely Christmas holiday."

"It was." He lifted her hand, kissed the back of her fingers. And then her wrist, and then leaned closed to kiss the inside of her elbow. "The most perfect Christmas ever. And I owe it all to you."

"Why to me?"

"Because you kept the family together when I couldn't. You took care of TJ when I wasn't there. You did the right thing for him and I will be forever grateful to you for that."

"I'm his mom. I'd always take care of him."

"You would, yes. Which is why I love you so much. You're my hero, McKenna. You're the one who gives me hope and strength—"

"Trey."

"And I might not be the man you always want me to be, but I am your man, heart, mind, body and soul." He rose up on his elbow, and leaned over TJ to kiss her, and kiss her again. Maybe it was the Cray in him, but he loved her the way he loved water and air, wind and rain, the sun and moon. "I think we made a Christmas memory," he murmured.

She smiled against his mouth. "And if we're lucky, a Christmas baby."

"Then it's a good thing we're getting married this week," he growled.

Epilogue

THE WEDDING TOOK place on January 1ˢᵗ, in the big Emerson barn, even though there were only thirty-five guests attending.

But it was a beautiful wedding, even if somewhat unorthodox with the bride in a 'vintage' gown that had been chopped off at the knees, the beaded bodice covered with a red flannel shirt tied at the waist. She wore red boots to match the flannel topper and carried a bouquet of lilies, red roses, and hay.

The groom wore all black—black trousers, black shirt, black boots—and a wickedly handsome smile.

There was a ring bearer, but the five year old grew restless immediately and chased his friends around the barn and ignored the adults who told him to knock it off, be good, and stand still.

The Douglasses were there, and Aunt Karen who didn't call the groom Satan or a Convict, which pleased the bride to no end.

The Sheenans were all there, too, including Callan Carrigan who delivered the shocking news that the five Sheenan boys had two Carrigan half-sisters, thanks to Bill Sheenan's decade-long affair with Bev Carrigan. It wasn't easy to hear, and it stirred up the past, but no one could blame Callan, and they'd all known her for so long, since she was just a baby.

There were hugs and a few tears, and then dinner, music, dancing, and cake, too.

But most of all, there was love.

So much love.

Because after all, what God had brought together, no man could tear asunder.

THE END

From *New York Times* Bestselling author
Jane Porter comes…

THE TAMING OF THE SHEENANS SERIES

If you enjoyed *The Kidnapped Christmas Bride*, you will love
the rest of the Sheenan brothers!

Christmas At Copper Mountain

Book 1: Brock Sheenan's story

The Tycoon's Kiss

Book 2: Troy Sheenan's story

The Kidnapped Christmas Bride

Book 3: Trey Sheenan's story

The Taming of the Bachelor

Book 4: Dillion Sheenan's story

A Christmas Miracle for Daisy

Book 5: Cormac Sheenan's story

The Lost Sheenan's Bride

Book 6: Shane Sheenan's story

Available now at your favorite online retailer!

ABOUT THE AUTHOR

New York Times and USA Today bestselling author of fifty romance and women's fiction titles, **Jane Porter** has been a finalist for the prestigious RITA award five times and won in 2014 for Best Novella with her story, *Take Me, Cowboy*, from Tule Publishing. Today, Jane has over 12 million copies in print, including her wildly successful, *Flirting With Forty*, picked by Redbook as its Red Hot Summer Read, and reprinted six times in seven weeks before being made into a Lifetime movie starring Heather Locklear. A mother of three sons, Jane holds an MA in Writing from the University of San Francisco and makes her home in sunny San Clemente, CA with her surfer husband, Ty Gurney, his vintage cars and trucks, and their two dogs.

Visit Jane at JanePorter.com.

Thank you for reading

THE KIDNAPPED CHRISTMAS BRIDE

If you enjoyed this book, you can find more from all our great authors at TulePublishing.com, or from your favorite online retailer.

TULE
PUBLISHING

Made in the USA
Middletown, DE
21 August 2023

37078653R00123